BIG OF YOU

ALSO BY ELISE LEVINE

Say This: Two Novellas
This Wicked Tongue
Blue Field
Requests and Dedications
Driving Men Mad

Big of You

Stories

Elise Levine

A JOHN METCALF BOOK

Biblioasis
Windsor, Ontario

FIRST EDITION
10 9 8 7 6 5 4 3 2 1

Library and Archives Canada Cataloguing in Publication
Title: Big of you : stories / Elise Levine.
Names: Levine, Elise, author
Description: "A John Metcalf book."
Identifiers: Canadiana (print) 20250152142 | Canadiana (ebook) 20250152185
ISBN 9781771966924 (softcover) | ISBN 9781771966931 (EPUB)
Subjects: LCGFT: Short stories.
Classification: LCC PS8573.E9647 B54 2025 | DDC C813/.54—dc23

Edited by John Metcalf
Copyedited by Chandra Wohleber
Designed and typeset by Ingrid Paulson

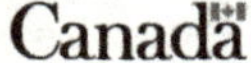

Biblioasis acknowledges the support of the Canada Council for the Arts and funding support from the Ontario Arts Council and the Government of Ontario, including through the Ontario Book Publishing Tax Credit and Ontario Creates.

PRINTED AND BOUND IN CANADA

For VS and JM

Contents

Arnhem

My husband leaves—I asked him to, or I didn't, I can't keep it straight—and I'm thinking, two girls on a hill. Heidelberg, or Conwy in North Wales where there's also a castle. Two girls, telepathic as ants, making fast along a wet street. Oxford or Bruges. One girl's freezing in her white summer dress. The other girl's clad in army surplus pants and a baggy turtleneck sweater. Both of them seventeen, smug as cats, having blown off the archaeological dig on Guernsey, for which they'd secured positions six months earlier by mail. Mud labour, fuck that shit. On the appointed start date they simply hadn't shown. Instead they thumb around, do all the things.

In a fancy café in Brussels, they order frites, which arrive on a silver platter, grease soaking into the paper doily. North of Lisbon they sleep on a beach one night. They run out of money in Paris and panhandle, not very well but they get by.

Who do they think they are?

Who did I?

I think we went to the zoo in Arnhem. I think we met a composer at some youth hostel who was from Arnhem. We met two young Italian men at a hostel in Mons. No one else was around and they tried to kiss us near the bathrooms when we went to brush our teeth that night. One of the young men forced one of us against the wall of the repurposed army barracks and thrust his pelvis a few strokes, while the other man stood back with the other one of us and watched. One night in the hostel in Amsterdam there was a phone call for one of us, and we both trundled barefoot down the stairs to the hostel office in our prim cotton nighties. Turns out one of our grandmothers was dying, the grandmother of the one of us who still had a grandmother.

I was the friend. We were friends.

I slept beside her in a roomful of older young women, all of us on cots half a foot off the damp floor. This was Cambridge. Dew on the windows all night, late June. The women were real diggers, by day excavating a nearby pre-Roman site. The men diggers, including my friend's older brother who we were visiting, and the reason we'd dreamed up the scheme of ourselves volunteering on a site, slept in another large room, down the hall—so much for the men. But the women—solid, practical, tough. Intimidating to the extent that when I say I slept, the truth is I barely did, cold, legs aching, bladder wretched because I was too scared to get up. To be weak. To even think it. Be that person.

Which one was I?

Not the one in the summer dress. The one in the Shetland turtleneck.

°

If I were telling this to my husband, I'd say: the next morning in Mons the sky was clear. Awake for much of the night, my friend and I rose early and packed and picked through the continental breakfast array in the main hall. Individual portions of spreadable cheese wrapped in foil. Crisp rye flatbreads. Ginger jam. I'd never seen anything like it. The Belgian couple who managed the hostel, in their mid-thirties probably, kindly asked how we'd slept. We spilled the beans about the young men and the couple's eyes grew round and their foreheads pinched. They would have a word with those guys.

By the time the couple did, if they did, and it's true we believed them, my friend and I were gone.

°

We left Lisbon broke and caught rides up the coast. Mostly guys, some with their own ideas. Sometimes a woman who'd ask if we were okay. We were okay.

°

The beach was small with large-grained sand. We didn't bother to take our shoes off.

The man who drove us there was slight of build. His mustache was light brown. At dusk he parked on the street and led us down to the water where we thanked him and said goodbye. He'd asked if we wanted to sleep on a beach that night and we'd said yes, please. Anything for an adventure to recall later in life. To say, How cool was that?

The sea frothed at our feet and the air smelled of brine. We toed a few half-circles and the sea erased them. We stretched our backs, yawned. He refused to take the hint. Thank you, okay?

He made himself understood then. He was spending the night with us. He'd called a buddy from the roadside café he'd taken us to earlier, where under his guidance we'd eaten squid in black ink very cheap and drunk cheap wine. Soon his friend would be here to meet us too.

It's not like the driver had a tent or sleeping bags. Was there even a moon that night? There was a family camping nearby. A woman, a man, a child maybe eight-nine years old. They had a tent. Sleeping bags, no doubt. Judging by the track marks, they'd dragged a picnic table over, and the fire on their portable stovetop burned brighter while the sky grew darker and the man and my friend and I sat on the sand waiting, he for his friend, my friend and I for some notion of what to do, clueless as sheep.

It grew dark-dark. A flashlight made its way toward us. It was the woman. With her nearly no English and our no Portuguese and a little French between us, she ushered my friend and I into the tent with her husband and son.

How did we all fit? I must have slept the sleep of the dead, for all I can remember of the rest of that night.

°

When we first got together, my husband complained I slept like a swift. When things went from infrequently to occasionally bad to totally the worst between us, he said I slept like a fruit fly.

I pull the covers over my head. He's not here to stop me, he's at a friend's—his, not mine. A week since yesterday. Good thing I brought my phone with me, light in darkness, all that. Especially with the news bulletins the past few days. Will I be okay? Will he? I hit his number and hang up when he answers. He immediately calls back, probably to yell, and I press piss off.

I ferret my arms out from beneath the covers. Stop calling me, I text-beg. Please.

For the next hour, while I still have my phone on, and for the first time in several years, he does as I say.

°

Around midnight I run a bath. I'm thinking again about the beach in Portugal, the family's tent—the next morning my friend and I woke and stretched and crept back out. The driver lay curled like an inchworm on the sand near the waterline, no friend in sight.

He did drive us back to the highway, game of him. We girls, young women, once again stuck out our thumbs. Auto-stop, they call it there.

I switch off the bathroom light and climb in the tub for a long soak. My phone is still off, but I've got it holding down the toilet seat, in case.

My husband is in IT. He's never once in his life hitchhiked. Like never even tried? No, he said on our first date, dinner at a pasta bar before a movie. Pale noodles, pale sauce, what can you expect for Cleveland, I thought, having recently moved there for the second of what turned into a seemingly endless stream of visiting assistant professor gigs. Before adjunct was what I could get. Now, not even that.

Like not even once? I'd pressured him that night over dinner. Never ever?

My date—who became my husband, at least for awhile, if I understand his intent by hightailing it to a friend's, if I understand my own intentions—said no in a way that I knew to shut up about it for good.

°

Before he left us that morning by the side of the highway, the Portuguese driver tried to kiss me. I bit his lip to stop him. Where had I ripped that idea from? Some movie or book.

He got mad. Pushed me from him and fingered his mouth. Looked like he was considering options.

Later, in the back seat of our next ride that day—a Spanish couple returning from holiday, non-English speakers—my friend turned to me and said, I thought he was going to hit you. Why on earth would you do that?

I shrugged her off. But I'd also thought he was going to deck me. Some memorable story, one for the ages, something to one day tell the kids.

o

Weeks before Portugal, immediately after the phone call at night to the hostel in Amsterdam—when my friend learned her grandmother had cancer, and might not make it, and I took this news in grave solidarity, assumed a mournful expression that said I understood, I was by my friend's side forever in all things—we sat on the floor outside our hostel room, nighties tucked around our legs. The old woman. The fights she fought with my friend the raging vegetarian, she of the curly hair she refused to tame. The stubborn fact of the fierce old creature—gone? Weird to think. But I nodded, weird I knew. The previous summer my father had an affair, and my mother told me about it, and now I told my friend about it. How the woman called my mother on the phone and said she and my father were in love. You're only in love with his credit cards, my mother told the woman.

My friend put her feet flat on the hostel floor and rocked back against the hallway wall, she laughed her ass off. My god, she gasped. What a stupid cliché.

Earlier on the trip, fresh off the plane, well before we'd hit the road thumbs out, we'd stayed in London, and things hadn't gone so well between us. At Trafalgar Square, on our third afternoon away from home, my friend undertook a spat with me. Talk to me, she semi-shouted. You literally dumb bitch. You need to tell me what you're thinking, share your thoughts. Otherwise I might as well have left you at home.

The sun is nice today, the sun is too hot. Another beer, why not. Look at that old man over there. In Madrid, I told her I was afraid of morphing into one of the numerous homeless some day. You won't, she said airily, you have family, friends. This sun is too hot.

°

I will share this: after my friend's first suicide attempt, when we were fifteen and she was in the hospital over March break, I declined her single working mom's invitation to host me at their house so I could help my friend through this difficult period. Instead I went to Myrtle Beach with my parents and little brother. Every afternoon the sib and I rode the Monster, tentacled and huge, at the sleazy mini-fairgrounds down the street from our efficiency motel room. Mornings we crossed the street to the hotel that actually was on the beach and baked in the sun by the heated pool. We swam too, hotfooting across the sugar sand to plunge in the icy waters, before reverse scampering and jumping in the pool to feel our skin burn. What else? I got mild sunstroke on our last day. For six bucks in a tourist shop, I bought my friend a pickled octopus jammed into a small jar.

You bet it was expired. Worse, by fifteen my friend had already gone vegetarian. When I got back home, more red and blistered than tanned, I paid her a visit in the hospital, and presented my gift. The look on her face. The shapeless blue gown, the big bandage around her wrist.

This was before Europe. I had no excuse. It was before my friend told me, that night on the Portuguese beach—sitting on the sand beside the driver who spoke little to no English, waiting for his friend to arrive, and before the family with the tent rescued us, that time in between, when the scope of our situation was beginning to sink in—that I really did not want to lose my virginity this way. Believe her, she knew all about it, having lost hers that spring, in the sleeping bag she'd borrowed from me, so she could go camping with this guy from our history class. He'd been a child actor in popular TV commercials and evolved into a cute teen actor doing same. Years later, years after this night in Portugal, he became a handsome adult actor, with a dimple so deep it nearly cleft his chin, and portrayed a cooped up astronaut in a popular show, and penned screenplays about the world wars, assigning himself the tortured-hero roles.

The night my friend and I slept in the tent in Portugal, I hadn't heard the ocean waves, though they couldn't have been more than twenty, thirty feet away. I hadn't felt the pounding. Like I said: sleep of the dead. Those waves crashing closer, shuffling farther out, and neither my friend nor I possessing a clue about tides.

°

Ice cream? Don't mind if I do. Two in the morning, I eat standing at the kitchen sink. Something my friend and I used to do, while her mother and brother slept. Two spoons, two heads bobbing together, middle of the night, one bite, two. Good times. Just us, peering into the backyard darkness beyond the kitchen window, to see what we could see.

When I met my husband he had a lot of friends—still has, he could stay away from me for ages, plenty of couches out there for him to surf—whereas I, as I proudly pointed out at the time, had few. Still have. Some point I once tried to make about integrity, depth, soul.

And yet, when I met my husband, I hadn't spoken in ages to my friend from childhood and teenhood and young adulthood. Still haven't, going on twenty years now. What I do have are a few colleagues picked up here and there over the years as the job market dwindled.

Dwindles. Slim pickings these days, in my field. I'm history, pre-modern. Not exactly a booming business, and me with too much experience for some departments, and not enough for others. Though I remain committed, overcommitted, to checking the wiki daily for new job listings. News of who got what in the end.

°

After Portugal and Paris my friend and I returned to England. We were somewhere I can't remember when she received a letter from her brother. Shane, the dirt-digger. Older than us by five years. An art major back home. Soon to become a prominent archaeologist, though of course my friend and I hadn't known it at the time. Since childhood I'd had such a crush on the guy. Oh, Shane! We must have been somewhere we'd planned to be, for her to have received mail. For her to pounce on it, rip open the envelope, and learn he'd acquired a girlfriend with a cute Scandi accent, and he was writing *expressly*, is how he put it, to let my friend know.

Next thing she was gone. Took the train north to meet up with him, having instructed me to stay put until she returned, and could let me know what was what. Like I even knew what that meant, or might mean.

I wandered the quaint streets of this somewhere-town for two days. For meals I bought glass bottles of milk with the cream on top. I leaned over the railing above a river where sticks rushed by, stirring the foam. Late on my second afternoon, a man approached, middle-aged and trim. I like your colours, he said, pointing to my army surplus pants.

He asked where I was from, and I shook my head at my boots. He offered to treat me to a pint at the pub, he was Irish, and did I know about the Troubles?

This was pre–Bobby Sands, and very much IRA and terrible violence on both sides, many sides. Even I understood that at the time.

The man went on to like my hair, near black, and long. And how old was I?

On a crowded street I finally dodged him—even though I liked my colours too, or thought I did, or didn't know what I thought. Except for knowing that he wasn't who I should ever tell any of this to.

On the third day my friend returned with not much to say. A new set to her jaw. We took ourselves to a sour-smelling pub for pale ales and a silent, shared packet of crisps, and from there, the next day, to North Wales, exchanging even fewer words, except to point out the stupidity of a young woman at a hostel near Snowdon, who'd washed her hair with a bar of laundry soap, so much for her flirting with the handsome young guy from Greece. We returned to

London, where we noted the prevalence of sporting dogs, silky with hauteur, on tony megacity streets. Even their panting pink tongues seemed swish, we declared, swish, trying the word on for size.

°

I hunch over my phone and ignore the news, scan the socials, check the wiki for new job prospects. No news from my husband. I work the search engines for signs of my old friend. No trail. Except her dad died three years ago, according to the online obit. It's true I have no intention of otherwise getting in touch.

Not exactly stalking, I exhume her brother. He really did land on his feet. The fancy archaeology post overseas. The tsunami of co-publications. Frequent international travel to oversee far-flung digs. Generalized acclaim at laying bare the historical record with his Danish-professor wife.

Some kind of trick mirror. His illustrious career. My friend, no trace.

°

What's my point with any of this? What was even the point of us. We who believed we could make ourselves into who we wanted, and that life would bless us in complicated, interesting ways. Does it go without saying? She'd fucked me a few times when we were kids, and a few more times when we were sixteen, before she gave up on me. Replaced me with that sharp actor guy.

°

Before I stopped speaking to my friend for good, she had a baby. We were twenty-two. The little one was born hardly that: it arrived late and enormous, scratching itself in the womb, and requiring my friend to have an episiotomy, and its poor wailing self, umbilical cord wrapped around its neck for its first appearance in our world, to be airlifted to a major research hospital, and placed in an incubator alongside the high-risk preemies. My poor friend. Stuck in another hospital, in the burb in which we'd grown up, and where she and her clueless-seeming, prodigiously weed-smoking spouse were raising weedy vegetables in a commune and studying social work.

I took the bus from our native, neighbouring city with her mom to visit the newborn. Two hours past drab fields under a grey March sky. This woman had been like a second mother to me, when my own was melting down over my father's cheating ways. The bus bumped along the highway, and this good egg asked if I'd never thought it strange how close my friend had been to her brother, when they were growing up. The brother who for years I'd had a massive crush on—did he like me, did he not, didn't, did. Years of this.

I turned my head from the streaked bus window. My friend's mom's face twisted, her eyes searching. I smiled to reassure her. Strange? How do you mean?

°

How had I missed it? A few years after the birth of her daughter, and not long before my friend and I said goodbye one night on a downtown street corner, really goodbye, we shared a litre of garbage wine at a noisy café, and at one point she leaned her elbows on the checked tablecloth, her face so familiar to me, more so even than my own, and I knew something was coming, something I wouldn't like. My heart sank. For sure she'd tell me.

When she did, I remembered the strange question her mom put to me on the bus.

You must have figured it out ages ago, my friend finished her declaration with. I mean, big duh.

My friend, her brother: lovers, once upon a time. I imagine my eyes grew round, forehead scrunched. Myself in some movie. How a person should react upon stuff finally falling into place. Cue the close-up, strike the bittersweet chords. Imagine me saying, Are you okay? Am I? Who ever is? Questions like headlights searching empty pastureland, rows of corny corn. Or driving on, just passing through. Like me, whose superpower it was, is, to nod and shrug and gaze into outer space. Coast by.

Then she was on to the actor guy, her undying crush. He was so great. Tim, oh, Tim! I needed to give him a chance. I needed a new hairstyle. I should never wear dresses. They made me look like I could easily be knocked down.

Then she had to run. The baby, oh Christ! she needed to get to the daycare and pick up the baby.

My friend's life changing in important ways. Not like mine, apparently—not given the scant extent to which she asked about it.

°

Not that I've ever wanted a baby. Not that she ever asked. But couldn't she have? And if not, why not?

°

My husband was, is, another case. He wanted. Wants.

Leaving me to my confusion with tense.

Especially when it's a new morning—okay, more like half past noon when I rub the sleep from my eyes, only to behold my husband, returned to me and standing in our living room, another piece of carry-on luggage in tow.

I lug myself to a sitting position on the couch. I wish I'd put on a cleaner pair of jammies last night.

It's your decision, he says, face pale.

I slip a finger under the elastic waistband of my bottoms, give a scratch to the not-quite belly mound. I resist the nonsensical urge to again look at my phone.

I can't hear you, I say.

His knuckles whiten on the grip of his roller case. It's true we've been nomadic, living in this city and that, Cleveland to Guelph to Charlotte, fruit of my now-diminishing spate of visiting positions. Unbound, too, by his ability to work remote.

My husband has never hit me. Never would. Will—should he return to me for good. Should I ask him to return to me. Hand out, begging him not to aim his Corolla toward points west, friending along, escaping my not-calls, until salt tides bear him far enough away that he can make peace with us on some strange shore I'll never know.

I can't hear you. I can't hear you. My mind on lockdown. On what is the danger here?

Marianne, he says. You never fucking do.

°

I know I'm supposed to move this whole thing forward. Not go back, string things out. Beg the past for ideas, even a single good one, for what comes next. At the zoo in Arnhem, a giraffe ate leaves from a tree, neck stretched over the walkway. Oh, giraffe! We walked beneath it, my friend and I, and heard the swallow taking the long way down. In Arnhem we drank beer and studied our maps. Where we might go. Auto-stop, that's how we'd get around. That's how we did. It's not so, it wasn't, so complicated. Auto-stop.

Cooler

I. CASINO

I interview Friday afternoon, Saturday morning buy the pants—those pleats, that crease. The wedge shoes with arch support, and a good thing too. That night I clock miles over the blue-and-gold carpet, resting the dogs only in the marble-clad stalls of the ladies' restroom where I briefly lose the clanging slots, the high roller's yips and groans—one of my new job's perks is that I never have to steal away to the basement and bless the employee can.

I learn fast: no strolling or loitering when a player runs serious hot. Dan or Gustavo or Cynthia tips forefinger to brow, and I amble over to the big table and ask in. Don't let on that my chips belong to the house. Strike up an unassuming convo with the rocketeer and dampen the sparks. Not that I'm cheating or distracting—my mere presence does the trick.

Nothing crackles from me. My luck? Failure to win. Killjoy, my parents taunted whenever the fam played crazy eights, and I cried over my starter kitty of ten pennies going and gone. Sad Sack Samantha, Mom and Dad would jeer. World's sorest loser! By age ten I knew that stoic resignation was my best, if not my only bet.

Until I met Deb and leveled up. Got my awareness raised.

My one and only old flame. She who trafficked in multidimensional, high-frequency attunements and how they flow. Or don't, in my case.

I miss her. She failed to tear my heart out, but it was complicated, nonetheless.

We met-cute one rainy afternoon two weeks ago. I, assistant stockist at Shop Smart, twenty-four years of age, newly barely degreed in business comm with a marketing concentration and so with little hope hoping to move the dial on my fortune in the world, uncharacteristically threw caution to the wind and abandoned my post stacking gum and candy bars to help her at the self-checkout. She was something, in her purple T-dress and yellow flip-flops and crystal pendant necklace, and I don't know what came over me—some sudden notion I had to for once seize the day. *Carpe diem* ironically coming easily to mind, being my former high school's motto, which pretty much had never pertained to me. Out of nowhere she pulled an eerie pre-empt by asking me out for matcha when my shift ended. Me, matcha! In no time we were at the café next door in the strip mall, a place I'd previously eyed but, frankly, had been too intimidated to try. She reached across the wobbly café table to straighten my twisted collar and swore she could see my muddy aura spike pastel peach. A smidge, she said, nothing razzle-dazzle—she liked to keep things real.

That very evening we spooned on her couch—spooned!—and straightaway it was all hard on me, not what I was used to. Winning for a change. It made my jaw ache, my feet itch.

What's up? she asked when I crawled onto her carpet and curled on my side. I spilled the uncool beans. She sat up straight with her arms folded and a frown on her face. Maybe slip into something more comfortable? I shrugged off my shirt—it did take some coaxing—and she disappeared into her bedroom and returned bearing a satiny bathrobe, freshly laundered, she explained. I donned the garment, but I who found it taxing to make it to my neighborhood Soap Opera Quick Wash once a week immediately succumbed to the worst rash. A soothing shower? At her urging—try a new look for the new you!—I ran her blow-dryer to straighten my habitually tangled curls, and clumps dropped to the floor.

Forget stoic. I moped. I cried. I lost sleep that night and the next—downgraded to a miserly seven hours a night. So much for new, I moaned.

And so three days into the cuddle-doves she announced her imminent departure on a never-coming-back-from trip. Which she kindly claimed she'd been planning to do for awhile. Something about needing desert and red rock and starseeds and the alchemy of ascension to salve the damages a lifetime of betrayals and poor-sportness had done her—the latter an attitude I apparently owned. Wounds I'd neglected to fix.

She told me this huddled over kombucha shots at the café I now—on this my second visit, pre–my next shift at the store—considered our place while I studied the green gunk on the inside of my glass. Go ahead, she urged me in a tone so sweet my teeth hurt. Get your grump back on, she understood, no way would she take it personally. And did you know the local casino could use help like mine? Which, alas, she could not.

Customers came and went, placing orders at the counter, hefting hips onto stools by the window, which looked out onto the mini-mall's parking lot, people parking, departing. All was motion, change. Except I couldn't move. Could. Not. She took my hand, which felt like someone else's. On second thought, it felt like just mine. Like how mine always felt—like it was embarrassed to belong to luckless me.

She flashed a smile big on the gums, and I revived enough to tell her no worries, it was okay, I got it. Her smile sagged, and she sighed and said the rest would be her one-way to Phoenix. Whereas you—and here her voice took on this whispery, seer-like tone that quivered the hair on my arms—you, Sad Sack Samantha, Wilmington-born and -bred, will forever stay.

And it was revealed: at least I had a gift I could cash in.

°

With my third paycheque I bankroll more perma-press. The months pile on, and the sensible shoes wear out, but I never mess with the style. What works works. A year clicks over and, still thinking of Deb—the hippie drama with which she dressed, her free-spiritedness—I brave a splash-out. The blouses upgrade from cotton-poly to lyocell, beige to pale pink and royal blue. Everything no-iron, but no prints, no way. I hold my breath—and keep my job. I add in the aspirational knock-off purse. Spring for clear polish on the nails. Hair done a medium wavy bob that covers the bald patches from my unfortunate episode with Deb's dryer, then every six weeks a lob back to bob and so forth, with humble highlights kicked in.

Not that anyone will notice. Which is the point: that I fly under the cosmic-vibe radar. Which is tough. Herein lies my dilemma: it sucks that my job suits me like silk. That my modest good luck, being my kind of luck, might scram.

°

Minutes to midnight on a royal-blue Tuesday, I've just returned from bathroom break, and there at the blackjack is something so far-out I wonder if even Deb could have foreseen it.

The auburn hair in a loose updo. Fat onyx studs agleam in seashell ears. A gauzy red capelet floating about the shoulders of a black sheath. The silvery laugh at each blown hand and shivery hiccups upon tossing back each comped drink. At each fold, the clapping like a kid giddy on Kool-Aid, the bracelets circling her wrists offering a festive tambourine shake.

She's down three grand. Five, seven. She's grand. Even Gustavo smiles.

I keep it cool, as per my job. A crowd has gathered, but really, what's the deal? Is she not just another loser, just like me? Maybe on a more exalted, next-level loser scale—a whale of a loser—but so?

I keep it sour. How come she gets to live so large? When here I am, months into antacids for dinner at my growing fear that each treasured work night might be my last. Odds are things will go south. I can practically count on it. Worse—something to do with the whale, I think, near-hypnotized by a certain pull on me, this tightening, lengthening, this perking in parts including but not limited to my heart and that I try my best to ignore, woefully aware of the little that's ever come of the experience—I find myself momentarily helpless to recount a representative sample of my lifelong chill-pills.

Deb's piled-on pity at Karma Kombucha, for one. For two: Franny Taggert's snort when, at age twelve, trying to impress her, I split my lip from a botched twirl at the skating rink. For three: why not Danny Rogelman's *Fat chance* piped at me in front of our tittering grade nine French class after I slipped the note asking him to the Wonder Winterfest dance. Four: in college, Maya Chu's toothpaste-y *What the?* when I nuzzled her ear at student union movie night—Bergman's *Persona* ever since reminding me of a two-mile solo return slog through freezing sleet to our cinder-block dorm.

Do I know cold. And while I break my heart again for each old time's sake, the whale burns wads with such joy a damp I'm-okay-not-okay fire swamps my bones.

At five in the morning she finally packs it in. Just as I'd bet she would, lays upon the dealer one lit tip.

°

For days I hardly sleep, and nights she's a no-show until Tuesday rolls around again, and, still on the job, I'm witness to another whale of a show and the crowd she draws.

I survey her table from afar until I can't take it any longer—her air of victory at each triumphant loss, the brutal thrill that now streaks through me—and go warm a seat in one of the fancy bathrooms, checking off-brand sales on my phone while randos shuffle in and out of the surrounding stalls. Which kills me. I have all the feels and all the questions, but such is life when the whys and hows are not for pity-parties like me.

The end of my shift finally draws nigh. I figure the coast might be clear on the floor, the crowds hushed back to their homes, and I flush and open. There she is, exiting the stall next door.

We stop short and stare. Is she tall. Gangly arms and legs poke out of a swingy, swirly colour number. I realize from this close up that she's too damned thin. As if, despite her élan, her writ-largeness with the big flop—because of the cost such brio exacts?—something's superwrong.

I think: warm plates of box mac-n-cheese, steaming bowls of instant ramen. Dishes I can sort of cook.

I think of Deb and offer a split-second prayer of gratitude for her role in leading me to this moment—an instant in which I'm also aware I might never think of Deb again.

The whale flirt-tilts her chin, as if she can read my thoughts. Heat rises in my throat and face—not entirely pleasant. Okay, somewhat pleasant. Very confusing. Me, blush?

She raises a bony finger to her lips. Between us, she says.

°

I clock out at seven in the morning and by seven thirty we're holding hands in the front seat of her Fit. Having made out, sort of, given the size of her car. Something unfamiliar bubbles in my gut. I'm—what am I? What is she? We? Happy as—

Candy? she says, withdrawing her hand to offer a breath mint.

We chew and suck in silence, then she starts the car and pilots us out of the underground lot. Leaving my ancient Sentra's fate to the mercy of the towing gods, who usually can't resist harshing those of my ilk, but I'm all, what, me worry now?

Twenty minutes later, she pulls over in front of my apartment building. She leans over and kisses me once more. My chest thrums, my head, between my legs. She is a mystery at heart, and so am I. And it's cool. And maybe I'm cool—first time for everything—until a freak niggle hooks me, a tiny insistent worm and, dumdum that I am, I bite.

Where's it all coming from? I ask.

The money is what I'm thinking—blundering past my churning thoughts of sex, power, powerful sex, me and her forever. Blindly thinking more, in this moment—in accordance with the tedious precepts of my schooling—of how to make the stone-coldest buy-in of my life.

She withdraws into her seat and forward faces. Um, yeah, she says. Just some clients.

I should have known: as if I could press my luck, as if I had her buckets to spend. Now I can count on the big N.O. to my as-yet-unasked question, the one about coming inside—never mind my studio sublet's a hazmat zone. The big ask with the oversized subtext: *Care to join me in fanning what might-could turn into an eternal flame?*

And yet my yearning soul remains split. *Clients.* The word orbits my brain.

How do you find these dopes? I blurt, figuring I've blown it with her anyway and now have nothing left to lose.

She studies me a long moment. A wavelet of excitement laps my throat. I gulp it in and, greedy for more, hold her gaze.

Oh ho, she says evenly. Easy, tiger. Not so fast.

I do it anyway—desperate now, I rewind, I show her fast, in full recognition of my initial breach. I'm sorry, my mistake, I get it—and when can I see her again? Movie date. Bistro dinner. Sunset stroll along the pinkening beach. Shelter for two under a single blanket while the horseshoe crabs mate under the full moon. No? No? Shared snoot of gin from a flask during my break next Tuesday at the casino. Side-by-side swings on the swings in a park in her neighbourhood—where did she say she lived?

She hisses a cold breath. Reaches across to open my door, arm grazing my breasts. I gasp, arch my back—okay, yes! I could go again, why not? But she withdraws her arm and nudges my shoulder, hard, with hers.

I shrink in my seat. Okay, I say. I get it, really, I do!

Though I don't, not any of it. Not me and her. Not the apparent business she's apparently in. But okay, okay. Okay! No argument from me.

She tootles off. I stand as if glued to the sidewalk. And then, within half a block, she hits the brakes and reverses with a squeal. Behind me a car horn honks, someone heading the right way along the one-way. The driver shakes a fist. The whale—my first, my only whale!—swerves even with me and buzzes down the window on my side while the car behind us wails.

I lean in. Grey eyes, somehow-elegant pimple to the left of her off-centre, regal nose. I wonder when she'd found time to reapply her red lipstick, the exact shade—I notice now—as her cape. Her lips part once more, and my breath catches like some creature—some hitherto hidden something, a thing I can't possibly know what— shocked to suddenly surface midair.

We're something, she says, as if she's sort-of, kind-of read my mind. Really something.

°

I snap the blackout curtains shut. Take off my pants and shoes and blouse. Hang what needs hanging and line up what needs lining, unusual for me. I pace in circles, a strange fizz in my fingertips, my knees. My tongue where it fished hers. Clients. Something. My brain burns. Between you and me. Like we share a secret, or we're the secret. And who would I tell—tell what? I lie on the bed. It spins—or I do. Like a roulette wheel—I can't help the cringey thought—twirling for all the little I'm worth as her red cape flutters in my dazed head. I press my own finger to my own lips. Somehow, they're spinning too. Also for all the little I'm worth—or is it, might it be, the more?

°

Two weeks drudge by, no whale. Such is my life, and such will it ever be: my upsides, my downsides.

Still, I order a half dozen shrink-wrapped twenty-packs of breath mints online, next-day delivery, and chew and suck as if they might return her. Two more weeks pass, then two more. And then two by two they come, until a year, and then another, sails past. I buy more same-old pants and blouses and shoes. But, and, I make a habit of hanging my things in the closet and aligning the condiment bottles on the fridge shelves. And it all looks pretty good—everything in its place. That third winter my hair grows out enough to entirely cover my bald patches, the ones from when I tried the blow-dryer in so-and-so's bathroom—I realize this sounds cruel, but who even was that anyway? And though, once again, I go about my days and nights slow and steady like I'm walking on eggshells, now it all feels like something, an accumulation of somethings that together might-could make a larger something, a thing that can't be rushed.

Until spring returns and I say duck it, purchase a slim-fit shirt with scarlet pinstripes—scarlet!—and hold my breath as spring roars to summer. And, defying fate, live to tell the tale. Tuck a sturdy grin beneath my professional, placid mien: job neatly done, that's my style. Risk believing I've at last bought a winning ticket in the lottery of longings.

A new year begins. At the casino the flyers up, up, and away on successive hands, the air thinning until they're north of nowhere anyone should ever be, in grave danger of losing themselves in the quivering frequencies of pure light—and it's okay, I've got them. I, their minty-breathed friend in time of need, lift too, swanning through the graces of my lucklessness by virtue of my mere proximity at the gaming tables, my lo-fi vibe enough to fish them back to a place not too hot, not too cold. Like me: just right.

Things look up in other ways too.

Don't ask me how—I'm a newcomer to this special game—but my best bet is word of mouth, insider knowledge passed along. Don't inquire about the long-term cost-benefit, keeping in mind the possible personal price my now-lost-to-me whale paid. Don't wonder where the blazes she went to in the end, if it was a case of she got out of the racket altogether or found fairer seas elsewhere. Just know that what's not to be beat is I'm needed and appreciated here.

Last night alone, on three separate occasions, players slipped me their business cards. A certain now-trending plea handwritten on their backs in tiny lettering.

Call, the clients-in-waiting implore. *Name your price. Save us, please.*

II. SPACE STATION

Star Date 2091.03.19 *Astral Hour 00.09.03*

From the time I was seven on a class trip to the International Intra-Agency's Ultimate Ultimarium™, I bought the whole deal. The cosmonaut's selfless striving in service to the knowledge commons. To humankind's urgent relocation needs. To the future, to progress! Not to mention the soulful calling in search of the spiritual benefits from the astounding elevation—from being out there and seeing Earth from above and apprehending the paltry truthiness of our personal concerns. From being up here.

Don't let this be you.

My name is Apple Montgomery, and I had hoped to make at least captain by now. But Shruti beat me to it, and after her accident Vinny the snake slid in—more on that coming soon.

For now, know that today, here on Pholus Sub-Central Superclass 8.2 Staging Nexus™—on the six-month anniversary of Shruti's transition, if *today* or *six months* or *transition* mean anything in a place like this—I am moved to take this matter of the gravest urgency into my own hands.

And so I begin my project of recording and then downlinking these secret logs to a secure location in an underground compound beneath a remote, mist-shrouded mountain on an asteroid in an undisclosed galaxy—at least that's what the brochure promises—for transmission to a new time in a new world. Fingers crossed.

To you forthcoming seekers and dreamers: don't be like me. Don't fall for the hard sell like I did.

○

AH 00:09:58

Time to bounce. Switching MainComm to PrivateChan, which will piss off Vince, but he can go—you know. Depressurizing—and open airlock—and exiting Hatch X-7 now. Hang on, let me swing my heinie around. And here we have it. Vast is no joke, a whole lot of nope, nope, nope. In the face of which it's keep calm and carry out the old instruments check. And check and okay. Heading now along Hull Y-5 to the Observation Nook in Lounge Chiron—almost there. And now what you're seeing is me torque-wrenching a loose bolt on the outermost panel holding the plex in place. Okay, mission accomplished, heck yeah. For my next trick, watch me loosen said bolt. Tighten, loosen, tighten. Fun, huh? That's not all I've got. Join me now as I peer in at the long mug on Dmitri, even more depressed than usual at parking his rear on the same stool every so-called day and partaking of yet another snack of dehydrated grasshopper, not even crunchy anymore, and our annual supply re-upping not due for three months. And that right there is the finger he gives when he catches me looking—so rude!

Sorry, but hey, it's the sorry show. Which is better than what's on in the other direction. Give me a sec. And behold: this boredom of stars, stars, stars.

And now, for your viewing pleasure, look what else: I can point and flex my toes. For real, no small feat performing space ballet in these big boots. Point, flex, point. And so on. Because out here, what is space-time anyway? An obsolete tick-tock in the inky everlasting. Point, flex.

Shoot, what you're hearing now is my EmergComm is what. Strap in—this too will be fun-not-fun.

Hey, gurrl.

That, my friends, is old-school Pittsburgh, should you happen to know some of the history of the place before it tanked for real in the Last Big FU some sixty years ago: the pretending to be someone else from somewhere else. Like Vince is hella cool in some damn hot place. Don't be fooled, like those Mission Control suits at Living Spheres Exploration™ headquarters on Earth, who panic-pushed putting a ring on the *Aye-aye, Cap'n V* as of six months ago.

As if I were the resident station zombie or something. As if that's why our fearless leader Shruti had to do the routine repair work. When how's about V or D? Like they were out there, here, every day. Like it was just me kicking back and letting stuff blow.

As if, ever since the accident, they're the ones kicking butt out here—as I do, on my own orders, thank you very much—to search repeatedly for stuff to do. And undo and do. And undo, and—okay, copy that. As in six brain-busting months of copy that.

Six. Months. The dividing line between when time still sort of mattered and now—whatever *now* means—does not. Mattered until spacewalking Shruti tore her suit and freeze-dried worse than the bugs we eat.

Apple! Come on and shoot some shit with me, okay? You okay out there?

To think I ever lip-locked the guy. Ran my hands over his sort-of four-pack back when we were all fresh out of flight school and—go team—together landed this seemingly plum commission. Back when, over the past seven years up until six months ago, V and I still bunked. When Shruti was still here.

°

AH 00:10:27

No really, I'm okay, okay? Don't worry about me. Because what is death anyway? And what the heck was Shruti even doing out there? Out here. Showing off her prole chops? When I could've-would've gotten around to whatevs at some point.

So her, though: to grub around like the rest of us, though she didn't need to. As if to say, *Despite my noble status as station overlord, I still possess the common touch. Dearest Besties, allow me to replace that screw.*

And then maybe her power tool slipped. It could happen, right? Even to perfect Shruti. Some gizmo accidentally slashing into the nineteen xEMU™ layers cladding her mortal flesh. The weaponized whatsis unrecoverable, released to the endlessness of the megacosm and the black holes of our surmise.

Sorry, here I am going for the lofty, getting all hopped up. But for real, I hope the tool scenario is how it went down. Because Shruti, man—despite or because of the effortless who-me?—was legit crazy cool.

Come the fuck on, Apple, I know you can hear me. You're done. Get your wrench-monkey ass inside, double-ASAP.

What I'm getting: as far from Vince and his recently cultivated trash stache as possible. He's been so on edge, impossible to live with. Ever since the whatever it was with Shruti on a so-called afternoon like any other: forever-frigid outside and boring-depressive inside, sick of each other's jokes after what's come to feel like a prison term of crewing together and the earlier years in training back on Earth. I, for one, seriously ill from the sounds of V clipping the hangnails at table in the dining compartment, and good old D non-stop belting theme songs from popular TV shows from the century past that are on permanent rerun and which we still sometimes slump around and watch. *Baby, maybe one more boom chaka boom there for you, yeah.* The clicking and belting twisting into earworms that riddle my sleep and snout fist-sized holes in my waking hours. I won't lie: my perma-crank a weather of its own.

Shruti, though. She never failed to keep things tight and not blur the boundaries, kept at the planks and lunges and spins on the stationary and regularly brushed her pearlies, continued analyzing the same old blah-blah data streams—as if they brimmed with new findings of paradigm-shattering import—and semi-religiously whizzed them back, as per schedule, to HomeBase™. She never, ever failed.

And the rest of us—having somewhere around year four chosen to believe our fate lay in succumbing to the sucking darkness—sort of resented her steadiness. Cold-shouldered her when she un-ironically, and with unfaltering bonhomie, bid us *Good morning, good night* every single putative morning and night until that pseudo-afternoon—after which she didn't, *yeah boom.*

Don't look at me. That swig, gasp, belch? More Vin, drinking his butt off ever since the ever-since, and probably there goes the last of Dim's vodka batch. And who'll be sorry then?

Not me. I have no sympathy. Because it was I who got to her first. That was me trudging way out by Hull Z-3. Which, by the way, I am now, taking you with. I know: more of same en route, this silver curve of the craft against peripheral-view curls of black matte prickled with these white sequin-y things, *très* tacky IMHO. But as I was saying: me out here, humping my bohunkus to the end of the line, heart in my trap. Me first with what was left of her. Not her. A wizened dummy imploding to dust when I clipped in and retrieved the remains and arked them through Airlock 7.6, and there was Vinny weeping on his knees. To give credit where credit is due. Vin panic-scrabbling loose the helmet, tearing the rest of the rig off, and trashing her suit.

Corp pay for an inquest? You think? Not on Shruti's short brill life.

And don't think for a sec that V and D and me didn't request Corp at least foot the bill to transport us to our once-blue sphere for some much-needed R&R before lighting us back up. Or better yet, that Corp send in the cavalry to whisk us home for the forevermore, replacing us wholesale with a newbie, more eagery-beavery crew.

We asked and asked. Okay, begged. And word swiftly back-channeled back to us, with a dash of reading between the lines thrown in. *Too spendy, too admitting things are a bust.*

Now it's all, *Come on in, App, talk to me, gurrl.* Whine, whine, whine. All talk. Though for real, we three leftovers never discuss what happened out there. Here, to Shruti. To the entire team before us on this very station who—according to rumours we glean from the oldie re-uppers before they tootle the fudge off as fast as they can—one by one undertook similar deeds. Some folks on the toss and others on the fetch end until there was no one left to play. *Oh yeah, that's right boom.*

Sometimes this is all I see. Weeping. Dust. No one offering me a stiff drink.

°

AH 00:10:42

X marks the spot. Point, flex. Flex, point. Not much to see. I mean, where were the signs? Regarding a certain best bud's hopping off the bus, if that's how it went down—like there was a burgeoning mass borne inside and deforming and creating a curvature, as per Einstein, in the old space-time of the self. If so, can another person just miss the clues, and how? Was it something this hypothetical someone did? Didn't do, did?

Other burning questions I have. Why make the choices we do? After we realize everything's gone to crud. Of what lousy stuff are we made that we want what we want in trembling fear? Did Shruti have her own answers? Despite, or because of, the rest of us. Because of me.

Is that last the worst I can think?

All these third-degrees these recent months. A long stretch, no matter how the mind slices and dices. A lengthy spell to carry on sad-sacking only to arrive—if I may go all circumlocution-y, as if one ever arrives when stuck out here—at this right here and right now exactly halfway conjunct Shruti's wish-you-were-here date. Which helps me contemplate it. Like she went somewhere great and is raking in the fab times.

To think we could have toasted her on this, her greatest success. Vodka shots all around—if the guys hadn't guzzled it all down. If I hadn't, okay, already polished off the gin.

We choose our own suffering. Of that I'm sure.

°

AH 00:10:53

Apple, hey! I still got some of these salted margarita bars. Last of my last year's stash. Just like Mama used to make.

Is it just me, or is there an echo out here? Never quits, does he? And like he really has those bars. Like his mama could even heat beans from a can.

I saved them, girl. Saved them. For—you know.

Stare with me a moment at the LowTemp Tile™ sheathing our once top-of-the-line ride while I practise my cooling breath pranayama. Because, for real, I'd like to race back in there and snap his head off.

It's not like I'm not aware: we're supposed to Learn a Lesson™. Make progress on Getting Back On Track™. Once a week our online VR-AI-PSYCH™ tries to give us a lift. *Go old-fash!* RoboShrink enjoins. *Write each other e-mems. Let it all hang out. See what turns up.*

I confess: I've given it some thought. In the spirit of the Corp's Try Until You Die™ mission statement, here's where I might go with mine.

Dear Vincent,

FWIW in my cold heart of hearts, I know what happened is everyone's and no one's and nothing's fault.

So I hope you can forgive me. Or at least forgive yourself.

As for me, what I've found is—

Sorry, but that's all I've got.

Yours (not really),
A

At which point or flex I might bounce from this very spot—unremarkable though it is to the naked eye, no monument or such like, such like being a standard reg no-no. I might well swing my arms into a breaststroke as if taking a day off to hang at the beach. Remember beaches? From the holos in Elementary PastEco Class? Colourful umbrellas, sandwiches in a Thermos bag. Dolphins and birds. Birds! So iconic. And a giant kite, and sparkling crests on the ocean swells. I remember. Shruti and me taking a VR-Go™ break before our final finals week at the Academy, Shruti laughing wide as the fake salt-gauzed sky, virtual sun flaring off her iconic, heroic-leader teeth.

For a moment, that's all I see.

She did like to laugh—until she didn't: *boom.*

°

AH 00:11:06

Sorry for the screaming. I hear it so on the regular I can now do V to a T: *Apple, get the fuck in here right now! Pretty please, App? Come on the fuck back in and see me sometime? Waah!* Who knew the pipes on him?

My *Dear V.* I just might go for it. Press send just to rinse the sound of him from my ears. Then go swimming out after Shruti. I'd be all, *Bitch, quit it with the teasing!* The endless *Girlfriend, that all you got?*

Imagine her back-talk! That I'd love to hear. It'd be like old times at school. The Quadrathalons and AstroJudo and Harmonitreeah Composition Competes when me and V and D would run our frisky mouths at each other and then Shruti would show us how things were really done. Show us up. And it was okay, we didn't mind. She was Shruti. The rest of us were just us. I was just me.

I wonder: where did it all go? The *Girlfriend, you want it, you go and get it.* The getting it involving unending streams of equations to solve for the steely joy of the ascent of our knowingness, that promise of deathless trajectory, eternal lift off. As if the stars were the foliage of a giant set design, backdrop for our prancing careers. Our grand show.

Listen to me here. Like I'm still all up on myself. Shoot—I'd be embarrassed, if I cared.

To continue: and then we blah-blah graduated and for awhile it was blah-blah okay. Until the pointlessness set in. Of endlessly orbiting this smol unexciting exo and unceasingly cooling our jets. So some maybe future cryo-voyagers could dock here awhile and unchill. Stretch their rubbery legs and resupply from our hub before reboarding and going under again and resuming their search for a new home for humans. And it'd be, *Thanks, been a blast, catch you on the rebound*—a joke. Their journey would be one-way. The ultimate selfless sacrifice—if there's one thing I've learned in my too-long life it's that there are always better-thans out there. If the grand endeavour ever even got underway in the first place. If the new bosses' bosses ever got it together and got game going for real instead of screwing around installing the rumoured newer better golf courses on their Self-Contained Island Reserves™ and inventing newer state-of-the art RoboSexers™ to cozy up to in their climate-controlled Sweetest Dreams Suites™.

Leaving we who once strove so hard stranded in this everlasting useless present where true belief—in the mystical value of productivity, in the conferral of status and the nurturance of self-worth obtaining solely from blood from a stone, in the form of slavish contributions to the inexhaustible supply chains feeding the endless growth-addicted interstellar money markets—goes to die.

I know, I know. She was my friend. I let her down. Our unit down. It's on my back. I get it.

Maybe I'll add a P.S. to my *Dear V.*

Not. YOUR. Fault.

°

AH 00.11.12

My last night on Earth, my proud parents clapped me on the back a few too many times and semi-joked that those early ballet and baton-twirling lessons had paid off. For real: where did it all go? The hot backyard evenings with little James in his nappy and me in my astronaut-print swimmies, no pool but the sprinkler on and the neighbour's sprinkler on next door and the neighbour's next to them, in a time when sprinklers and next-door neighbours still existed. And I, a diehard back then, studied the silver transits' cooling arcs across the airglow, their hiss navigating my brain as if sentient, a consciousness webbing me with desire—for a great destiny, travel across the firmament—and I pointed and flexed toe deep in damp lawn bordered by petunias, back when lawn and petunias still existed, albeit increasingly illegally. Me: back-bending, arcing like a taut bow vibrating with faith that I could rocket my seven-year-old's yearnings—for more ice cream, more semi-dreaming moments before bedtime, twilight bordering into the midsummer night, the hedges breathing green, the sycamore flicking its leaves and the last starlings of the day winging onto branches and settling, the swifts rising and bats too, all the rising and resting, only resting, the leaving and never arriving but the maybe arriving, the possibility of it—into a someday astral who'd kick out all the stops and perform to beat the band out there.

Up here, way out, where Shruti went. Far freaking out.

And here I finally am: looking straight at it. My grand future.

Only, I don't know? Push come to shove? I'm not a hundred percent it's looking back at me.

°

AH 00.11.17

I can't explain why I hang on. Why any of us do and Shruti didn't. Why she broke up with us in the end, calling curtains—and we're supposed to live with that? Not touch that dial, not change a thing.

If Shruti did what I and probs V and D on the down-low think she might have done.

I should mention: I'm not sure if whoever you might be will ever hear this. But just in case, strictly need-to-know, here's the real hot take.

My name is Apple. Apple with the questions, to which the answers prove pure mystery. Might as well quiz the dying Earth, interrogate the perishing Earth-life. Might as well sweat this perma-night.

Or go truly big with the ask.

Dear Captain Tomorrow,

Permission to speak?

Okay, so I wish I'd jumped on the aye-aye on the old whatevs—sorry for real!

And while we're out here, permission to some 'day' come 'aboard'?

And not just for me. For V also, in spite of his too-cool-for-schoolness, which annoys me no end, but it's fine. I'm fine. In the end, I get it. I'd be cool with all that. And D as well, mouth full of bugs as if he's already dead and buried in earth back on Earth, but I can deal. I get that too.

What I'm really asking: permission to untwist a few strategic bolts and thereby re-up the whole gang, all for one and one for all. Solid as—yeah boom.

Yours truly (for real),
A

III. ROADSIDE ATTRACTION

I bought the billboards. I am the one.

Not Anatu who raised my ancestral palace and lived two hundred years before willing its care to Hurin their elder, and not Hurin's thieving half-brother Aaron nor his half-brother Saul who together waged war and blight. And not Saul's beloved consort, Oona of the North, who helped seal the deal on his ill-gotten gains by getting the peoples on her side. Nor the winning couple's offspring Tippi nor Tippi's great-great-grandcousin by marriage Theodorus, who sold to upstarts loosely descended from the line who sold to those increasingly not, including Hilde, Erik, Vicky, Al. And Jerry—Jere for short. Who, a decade ago, scaled down and restored my digs continents away in this other desert, a new world. Where in recent times I have asked: what has Jere really done for me?

Yes, it is Jere who supervised the construction and cut the cheques. But trace it all the way back and behold, it is I who paid for the clean restrooms and ace AC system. I who paid for the gift shop with its unisex tees, my picture on every single one. I who purchased the voice-over artist to narrate the video presentation—very educational—and the preggers video artist too, green for five months' worth of grub in a two-fer I now own.

It is I for whom people stop. For whom they shell out the six bucks' admission. To gaze upon me.

Does it not follow that I bought Jere? Onboarded to build for me and promote. To bask in my glory, withstanding as it has civilization after civilization and species upon species crumbled to dust.

And for what? For Jere to lean over the cash register yesterday afternoon while thunderclouds boomed across the horizon and threaten me. Make like he will unload me on the eBay.

JERE: Dood, receipts are way down. Getting near time to slash and burn. Break up us bros.

ME (lips sealed in my patented millennia-proof snarl):

Now it is early morning. From my raised dais in the exhibit-slash-throne room, with my superpowers of perception I discern a salute to my beauty in the river of silver sky above my palace, in the uncountable hectares of golden sand scented with sagebrush. A redstart starts up, having journeyed from its riparian home farther west to pay homage—how the little bird sings! The silky jackrabbit slips from its burrow and sniffs the pomaded breeze. And when, in worship of my radiance the refulgent sun acclaims me, I accept while reclining in the GOAT indoor air that is my due.

If Jere thinks he can rip me from this sick life he has another think coming.

Desert dawns. They really get *me* thinking. This one more than most.

°

Ten in the morning, we've barely opened for business, and Jere burns his second one of the day. Warns me to peace out.

My skin would crawl if it were not so shellacked. For it is Jere who taught me more lingo and a few corresponding skills than I had learned in the previous four-five thousand years—and so Jere, of all humankind, should know that I know peace out, I know chill. I have chilled, if not all along then at least in these more modern times. Jere should know it is I and not Jere who knows how to read the temperature of a room.

Case in point: when my sensitive hearing pricks at the sound from our parking lot, I foresee exactly what will happen next. Sure thing, a van door wheezes open and out tumble little Tommy and Shonda with big bad bearded dad bearing down on them from behind, and in they come with their shrieks and dad-chuckles and need to pee in the comfort of the comfort station, their need for snacks from the gift shop, and cooling drinks. They approach my high perch, and the short ones' cotton-candy fingers sticker me despite the DON'T TOUCH sign mounted on the railing of my throne. Can the children not read? No, they cannot. No matter. I fuss not.

And what I really do not appreciate: smarty remarks from this basic husband whose basic bish wife—very disobedient, not with the plan—prefers to chill thumbing magazines in the car.

When I am the one, a different case, there is none other like me, who once fed contumacious, ruin-predicting court astrologers to lions and downy owl chicks to my three hundred duteous consorts, kissing plumage from their lips. And should a beloved choke to death of a morning's repast, by noon I soothed my grief with a stroll through terraced gardens of rare orchids or hand-fed one of the infinitely replenishable stream of albino elephant calves—which grew fast and then failed to delight me—sailed aboard oared ships and then transported by slave-hauled sleds across the burning dunes. Flower, calf: either way, so relaxing. And by evening the psalms of nightingales praised me from their gilt cages, revealing the divine embroidery of consolation: for me.

And not for Jere or Tommy or Shonda or the basic 'rents. Or—did I say?—Jere.

For I am undead, and they are not.

And it is hardly original when dood-dad takes a selfie with me and zaps it over to the better bish half who cannot be bothered to leave the vehicle and stand before me, quaking with wonder and awe.

DAD TEXT: Who's better-looking?
ME (twitching trademarked claws):

Though I have thoughts about this too. To be crystal clear: only thoughts. Which would kill me—if I could be killed.

The life of the mind: I live it if not always love it. And how is that for peace out? For chill.

°

And here are another think or three when, for a hot minute around noon, a rickety Greyhound pulls in, seeking respite from this planet increasingly in flames.

USUALS (piling out and beelining for my temple's frigid blast and, once inside, pulling damp shirts from chests, sweat marks fanning the seats of their shorts): Hoo, that's better! Damn straight!

ME (not even rolling my waxen eyes, not even when I overhear Jere ringing up some Deb's Funyuns at the register):

JERE: Phoenix bound, huh? I've got some buds there I hang with. You want, I can loop you in.

ME (as if he thinks cupidity does not rhyme with—):

DEB: What are you, Aquarius or something?

JERE (with a snap of his fingers): Snap! What are you, a mind reader?

DEB (chuckling): As a matter of fact—

ME (not even shaking my head, since it is true that although death's dominion is somewhat overstated—I alone am proof it *is* not for everyone—it is for normies such as Jere and Deb, and because death is def for Jere and Deb and, sooner or later, sooner with any luck, for little Tommy and Shonda, and not for me, and in my case luck has nothing to do with it, it is all in the genes that I am this striking, two thousand and ten percent original, first and last of my kind, huge with legend—for these reasons alone I, in my greatness, chill now, let the lesser be less. What, me worry?):

DEB (punching in a number on Jere's phone): Promise you'll give a tinkle?

JERE: So on it!

And it is okay, I chill, I deal, and soon the Greyhound rolls. Soon the coyotes will howl, and Jere will shuffle about spraying for scorpions, and tomorrow all manner of vehicle will streak by on the interstates and the most righteous among the peoples will pull off the road and come on in and offer me their astonishment, as is right.

But not enough will stop, not in these most recent times, according to Jere, so hard to please. Jere who, despite his chillaxing spliffs, has these past months—when months are nothing, not worth a comment, trust one who has survived millennia—has taken to stroking his long Jere chin and frowning. At me.

In all fairness: I do know less and lesser. I too feel the feels.

For truth be told: my ginormous and immortal form—way back in the Mesozoic replete with mane of cliff-tall spikes and delta-long electric-blue tail, eyes aglimmer like the antediluvian night skies, flashing crimson, alabaster, cerulean, on, off, on-off, the heavens back then code-switching for we motley of gods—did contract by half at the end of the last ice age. And since the worst passed over me, and mostly me alone, I, of mostly all beings, best understand extinction's a bummer, as Jere used to say in commiseration a scant decade ago when we were first partnering and still pal-like, the two of us upending the brews around the firepit out back into the wee hours, gassing on as we trial-ballooned ideas for nailing my brand.

About that last part.

JERE (excitedly waving his short Jere arms, expressing the vivacious young-buck life force he once embodied, now drained to zip): I know! I've got it! SAY WHAT?! That's what we'll call you. So great, right?

ME (shrinking at the thought but beneficently giving the benefit of the doubt, not wanting to be negative):

Anywhoozle, about my contraction: change is good, right? I am down with it, though it cause pain untold, I am with that program, it is not for nothing my once-supple skin is now crazed with cracks. I know change, I too have suffered, and not only during the last ice age.

For examples. When my fifty-seventh daughter became my twenty-third wife, I dwindled by another half. I could see it in the eyes of the peoples, thinking they had become so smart, high on their horses with the invention of morals and stuff-like, declining to bow before me as previously among the elegant cedars and gift me roasted gazelles innumerable, stuffed with ripe figs. And when my ninety-second son attempted to drown me, I waned, and again when I fed his liver to the crocs and, copy that, when fiery insurrection and pillage begat every manner of odious pestilence visited upon the land. And then Cousin Seth—related to Theodorus? I forget—stole my throne. And I, though much diminished, rallied my starving worshippers and beheaded his ugly ass, though he had once entertained me with his flute playing, his cracking of corny-ass jokes. And I did pine and made myself scarce. And anywhoo, grew sadder, and restive—in truth more bored than sad. And thus sold myself down ancient rivers to whoever could pay for a look-see.

And many aeons journeyed the ocean waves. And it came to pass, through treachery and abandonment, that on a scheduled two-day overstay in Venice, our mighty cruise ship tremoring to certain ruination-to-come the stone pathways and heritage villas, I needed to seek refuge at an overcrowded tourist-trap trattoria where, forced one afternoon to share my miserly bar counter footage, I got to gabbing with Jere over a consolation of seafood misto and wine, white and excellently cold.

And the rest is but more, though less interesting history. But the point is: I am down with change, for I rule now in excellent AC, the greatest of inventions—forget the overhyped wheel, so old news.

Now, in all fairness I will allow it is also true: eternity might be wow, just wow, but Jere does have a point—nowadays, too, it is sometimes doom and gloom. Especially with two cars and one bus a weekday, on average, stopping in. And weekends: with luck, a bummer of eleven vehicles total. And so sometimes it is a world of hurt that I, who am the one, worshipped once by all the creations, am in.

Especially when Jere gets out the shellac brush on Sunday evenings and gives me a too thorough going-over, and re-checks the wires wiring my jaw in place.

The things Jere says then.

JERE (red-faced and huffing in between chortles from the exertion as he, too, takes on a certain patina of age, except mortal and swift and far less glorious than mine): There you go, old boy. That should you keep you going for now. Or not!

ME (the now majorly miniaturized fifty-seven thousand valves of my heart nearly breaking all at once):

When it is I who have witnessed the splendour of the desert on the three continents, swum Earth's seven oceans and thirty-nine rivers. When for Deb and Jere and the skinks and Komodos and Burger Kings—kings! as if I should be impressed, should one ever cross my threshold—and the Yorkies called Brutus and Chihuahuas called Mister Big whose owners can't bear to part with them and, thus, carry like tiny panting tributes into my sanctuary, when for such as these it is death and more death. And though for now I keep a steel grip on my claws and merely grit these fangs, I cannot stress enough that, despite the pooch owners' gauche interest in cryogenics—and do not even speak to me of taxidermy, which I will never understand—death will come for all, including their cutie beloveds. Because death is still death. But not for change-positive but still-magnificent, non-fungible me.

It is for Jere. For what he said yesterday. Offering me to the highest bidder. Wiping the slate. Starting again from scratch.

When it is I and not Jere who have outlasted extinction. When it is I who will outlive. I who will show Jere scratch.

°

Late afternoon now.

Jere is counting the day's sad receipts and pulling the long Jere face, long as a donkey's, like he really is thinking of folding it all in and leaving me down in the dumps.

And I, in my great mercifulness, give Jere another chance, I try to explain it to Jere again: death is not for me.

> JERE (staring at my illustrious personage as if deep in nefarious thought, thin lips curled in a sneer far less fetching than my ferocious perma-snarl that, when we first met, he professed to really dig): Complainer.

ME (thinking Jere does not know that explaining is not complaining, nor does Jere understand that history takes time, it does not come cheap, it exacts a price, one must wait on it, and what Jere truly does not know is he might find himself very sorry at some point):

Now Jere locks the door.

He hooks his thumbs into his belt and death-marches to the gift-shop counter and opens the laptop with a hard flip. Showdown time, in the spirit of the new world desert in which I find myself—find that my time unending has come to this. Which is not chill. Not cool. Jere, fingers twitchy over the keys, but playing it cool, like Jere even knows what that really is, laying on the heartless in his refusal to now look at the glory that remains of me.

Speaking of. This elegant, human-child size. This mane a high-tide crest of dander-scurf. This potent, secret-sauce, fungal scent. And this recently acquired ambition for self-mastery, a trend far superior to the old-hat booyah I once exercised over every living and even dead thing. For example—killing two birds with one stone—when I uprooted the buried and of their bones commanded puppets be fashioned for ribald performances adored, or else, by my palace throng. Which enterprise—proving my point—I am so over, so been there and done that. So peace out now.

I feel for Jere. He refuses to gaze upon me but I, the greater of we two, the now more spiritually inclined, contemplate him. Apprehend the inner turmoil therein. The vicious and self-destructive need to self-assert, fingers a-scuttle over those laptop keys.

Speaking of twitchy. These claws, these fangs. If I weren't so chill, I'd say Jere for real needs to take a gander and understand, as I do, how tables can turn. How my most fearsome attributes—how the young ones enjoy squealing at the sight—remain a good look. Millennia-proof, I would say. If I could.

Dig!

FROM A

It's the next morning. I summon my strength and call my father's wife.

It's your daughter, she tells him, on speaker bedside at the nursing home. Your daughter! Say hi!

Each time she says *daughter* I lose a piece of my own mind.

He splices together some unintelligible sounds, their own language, one I don't know.

Dad has a new vocabulary now, his wife says.

I swallow a laugh. It's been a year—his previous birthday—since I last spoke to him, spoke at him. My guilt has gulped chunks of me and left a gummy residue like tar, but suddenly I feel light, unburdened. The moment I've been waiting for: having head-on entered late-stage dementia, he really can't remember me. Cue the credits.

He gives a good long gargle to clear his throat.

My first born, he growls, some loose line in his brain zipping tight, releasing a trapdoor-heat that yawns in my gut, base-of-my-spine kind of thing.

A shocker—this space I'd never noticed inside me, until now.

How could I? I think, suddenly appalled. Under what terms accept the gift of this anointing. An enlargement, a primal knowledge of how special I am. Might be. Once was.

Knowing I'll never see him again, I can't, no way.

°

After the call I catch a crowded *vaporetto* and cling to a pole, legs braced as the boat seems to churn up and down rather than forward and across.

My first time in Venice. One of my books has been translated by a local university class and published by a local press. As part of a conference, the university has been hosting me for a class visit and launch. Yesterday morning, I tried for sophistication in a fitted black dress and, clutching a glossy scarlet file folder containing bits of paper on which I'd scrawled an overcaffeinated thing or two to say, burbled some jet-lagged and possibly encouraging words at the students. I then stumbled through a lavish lunch, a mini-tour of the city, and awkward *aperitivos* in company with faculty and conference luminaries, dashing hopes I could impart anything remotely resembling smart bookish gossip, before I fled to my hotel, bailing on further attempts to be someone everyone seemed to want me to be.

Could I be any more tired? From the flight and time change, the overlubricated speechifying of others. My antic, flawed self-performance.

But it's mid-May, with perfect weather for an all-expenses-paid trip to the storied city. I take the bait and hang tight as the water bus motors apparently forth and at each stop people melt on and off. Another moment I've been waiting for: blissfully solo and determined to ride to the end of the line. And there disembark, to lose myself among the sinking treasures. Descend into shapeless pre-thoughts, as if tunnelling beneath art-choked, terrazzo-tiled *sale* and crumbling foundations. Grope through dank water and mouldy substrate to the other side of the dark, sonorous earth, and emerge in a disambiguation of personhood—to skylark, no questions asked or answered half-assed. To simply take in.

Or something like that.

Off the bow of the water bus, racing the sky-blue sky, a hawk. A thin line dangles from its beak. String. Rat-tail. Baby snake.

°

Late afternoon, I spy you—or a reasonable facsimile thereof—outside the Doge's Palace. You're hunched on a bench, unscrolling a map. Or blueprint, it looks like, and I think of honeycombed subterranean chambers stuffed with magnificent loot.

I slow. It really is you. Stocky build. Snub nose. Frizzy mane corralled down your back with a hair tie. The shaggy-beast resemblance.

I bite the inside of my cheek, but my surprise feels manufactured, stale. I've boredom-googled you over the years. You get around, it's your thing. Inner Mongolia, the Cape Verde Islands. Nepal, on the first-ever archaeological expedition to employ a local shaman. Some kind of joint project with the Tate Modern I can't figure out. Lots of European prehistoric and Roman with your Danish-professor spouse.

A damp breeze rustles your chart. You glance up and meet my gaze, and I nearly jump out of my skin. The ground cuts away from beneath my feet, my vision swims, all that—the moment feels unreal, movie time, cue the strings.

But I hang on, curious to see what next.

Your face, as full-cheeked as in your teens and early twenties, twists with hate.

Though it's been nearly thirty years, I walk on. That's my thing.

°

You carry me in your arms. Down and down the steep steps from the cottage your grandfather built, while I flicker in and out of consciousness, geraniums and birches and blue morning sky swiftly growing dark. At bottom you fold me into the back seat of the neighbour's car for the twelve-mile drive to the hospital, and I can hear the muffled, worried voices of your mother and sister nearby.

I've knocked myself out. Pre-breakfast with your sib, my best friend. The two of us fifteen going on seven and thick as thieves, capering about the crooked patio, mostly her chasing sidekick me. I fling myself from her lunging grasp into a rotting wicker chair and upend backward and headfirst onto a stone planter. Get up, shake and sputter until the black wings of tunnel vision sweep me away, and I crash for real.

I come to squashed helplessly against your torso, squeamish at this touch I've longed for throughout girlhood, having worshipfully conferred upon you the status of first hot crush. Crush I share with your fierce, fevered sister.

You must be twenty, captivating us with your presence on a rare long weekend off from your summer job stocking shelves at the liquor store back home in our dull burb, before you leave for the rest of the school vacation to tour Scotland, Holland, Sicily, Morocco, Spain. You've arranged to volunteer at your first dig, in Yorkshire, excavating pottery, coins, bronze tools, bones—I don't know whats—for evidence of settlements and trade routes. All spring your sis and I have worked ourselves breathless over your Captain Awesome itinerary.

The head injury is another first: of three concussions I'll go on to sustain. A mild one. I suffer an afternoon of rest, lightly brain struck. Unleashed from your sister's hectic, seductive masterminding of our days—a mostly welcome escape from the repetitive chaos of my home life. Free to wend my way through an unabridged *Moby Dick* in the cool shade of my bottom bunk, forbidden the sunny beach. Beyond the window, sunlight shifts aquatic through green leaves. In my rumpled white sundress, I drowse and wake. My body glassine, a clarion stillness. I am the whale, the words. Call me not Ishmael nor Melville, but by my own mask. My high hopes for the pages I'll fill.

I've already dreamed this future. Sort of dreamed. Ever since I first put crayon to paper, or to the drab walls of our cramped dining room at home—the latter assay followed by my mother's tears and fury, arms paddling my direction down the hall as she chased me for a good spank. I'd learned to stealth-cover my undertakings, rather than boldly proclaim them. Learned to blame my creations on my poor brother, a defenceless two years younger.

But at age fifteen, solo in my bunk at your family cottage, in the smuggled rest of a semi–sleep paralysis, for the first time I apprehend the certitude—though not the shape or material, not the truths, not yet the complexities—of my owned marks.

And then, that very night, a partying motorcycle gang shows up at the nearby bay front, just a few dirt roads away from this small cabin with no landline—this in the days long before mobiles.

By eleven o'clock your mother and sister and I huddle in silence by the sagging couch in the living room, while you stand guard at the picture window, gripping a splintery tennis racquet, peering without your glasses into the trees.

I feel for you then. Sorry for you. Embarrassed on your behalf. This recalibration, of my take on you, still another first: my recognition that you've been thrust into this great-protector role. First born and recently crowned man of the house, given your parents' recent separation—and now, in this very moment, you're plunged far deeper than in your morning rescue of me.

Honestly, what can you do if things truly go south?

A rustling of branches. My feet hover above the floor. My flannel nightie, stained with honey and butter and pineapple juice from multiple breakfasts, sways against my legs. The night air strains through the window screens like a living creature rearing tentacles of male laughter and glass breaking, engines revving—infinitely more alarming, and thrilling, than the usual nocturnal visits from raccoons bumping through the outdoors garbage cans for mouldy peaches and chicken bones.

My hair stands on end.

I can't say it's fear that grips me. Just this rising, a leave-taking. Like nearly falling asleep and knowing it. Another toggling back and forth between worlds.

Suddenly you tip your head toward us, teeth bared. The look—pure rage, as if we're the enemy—more like a smell, more bitter and chemical than sweat.

Inside me, a headlong shower of dust to dust, space junk. Then my bare toes grasp the hooked rug again, and I lock my knees.

°

In Venice, outside the Doge's Palace, I survive my first witness of you in decades—the death-ray you laser in my direction, even though I must be ancient history for you. As your sister—my long-abandoned, former best friend, recently dead of multiple myeloma, according to my recent search-engine searches—is for me. And must be for you, her long-ago hero, the hero she created and held fast to. Your sister who I left. And you left too.

I make it official: I am dead-done for the day.

Another *vaporetto* ride. Buffeted by the motion, the suffocating afternoon heat, the slither of diesel and canal stench, I slink off at my stop. Aftermath swarms of gold-framed virgins and saints—the entire La Serenissima Rococo sensorium—blitz my brain. Dizzying, these tall ancient buildings on narrow streets. Stone grotesqueries grin at my hairpins, stalk me through reeking people-less alleys that in my distracted state I hadn't noticed the previous day. Vanished are the tourist-trinket storefronts, eateries with signs promising American-style meals. Instead, piles of bagged garbage, dusty doors, seeming relics of centuries past. For what feels like hours, years, feet blistering in my expensive-folly sandals, I repeatedly end back at the sloppy water.

Is this how my father feels? Or used to, in the early, pre-diagnosis years of his memory malady. When his sense of where and who he was, his inner compass of self-awareness—never his strongest suit, given his lifelong narcissism, his inconstant moral acuity—hadn't wholesale deserted him. This self-vacating—is it coming for me? Already here? Given my history of head bangs, and scrupulous inattentions to dull everydayness—rehearsed until second nature—that conjure an away-ness I've come to rely on.

A taste of what's to come. A paying of the price.

For real, though—how lost can I be? I mean, come on. The map app on my phone might be useless among the warren of heritage footpaths, but I'm not brain-dead yet. I hope.

I bear down, as if reassembling each neural cell one by one, and creep each elbow turn and flare that leads inward from the canal. Until, legs trembling and with shredded heels, I crook around a corner and my hotel appears—not where I expected it to be, but opposite, in an inverse mirror image of the picture I'd held in my head.

I reach the hotel door. Sweat shivers from me. I reach for the ornate handle with my free hand, and it hoves into view, a chalk-white curio, an ancient find fished from unknowable depths—I exaggerate, so sue me—just as the youngish French translator from Lyon, who I'd met yesterday at the conference, is stepping out.

He blocks my entry, lifts his chin toward me. You again, he says.

I slip my sweat-slicked phone into my tote. Raise both hands toward my face and make a show of examining my lined palms, as if I were some dodgy chirologist. Turn my very middle-aged mitts over and scrutinize the well-established liver spots, the pronounced veins, their own twisty map. Yes, very middle-aged.

Guess so, I say.

He flicks an arched brow and struts off in his unwrinkled linen trousers and crisp white shirt.

Seated next to me at yesterday's lunch for twelve, he installed his hand on my knee without breaking stride in trumpeting his recent fancy-pants publications and august awards. I spooned more risotto into my mouth, polished my glass of wine. I smiled. It wasn't so hard. Nor did I experience a hardship in imagining his tongue in my mouth—trying the idea on for size. Take him for a spin? But I sat tight, not unable, but at bottom unwilling to decide yes or no. Why make the effort? I hadn't made the first move or next move, I'd made no moves, I was empty of the faintest interest in the shopworn trope, the hardly fresh experience of having some guy in a professional setting overstepping in my direction. I found myself pleasantly devoid of desire. Unpossessed by a flicker of interest in thinking more about me, me, what about me?

What about me? What did I want, what would I do.

The translator continued to hold forth while he inched his paw to my thigh, until our server removed our plates, and briefly tongue-tied the young Frenchman by proffering dessert. I couldn't care less. About any of it. The pleasure in my freedom from care deserted me, and I couldn't for the life of me be more impossibly, fatally tired. From the demands of this trip. From tired-ass me.

Do not get me wrong. I often dwell in this bleached territory of the soul. Slip into it when, somewhere in the wild woolly middle of a project, I can see the glorious or—more usually—inglorious end but can't figure how to get there. How to fit the parts together. Make them track. Every accursed time the same: my method requires me to shrink, increasingly wraith-like, humiliated, prostrate before a once-scintillating, now-become-shaky idea. In danger of vanishing into a terror of never finishing, sucked alive into a mega fail.

Where I am now, with this new story on my hands. This very one. And truly—truly—it's killing me.

Took a lot, but I held fast amid yesterday's tinkle of silverware, and the translator's immodest and, I admit, seductive confidence. I resisted the urge to leave my napkin discreetly and invitingly draped over my groin, withstood the urge to attempt an alluring dab at my oiled lips with my fingertips, and with a subtle arch of my spine imply the whole why-not shebang. To see what would happen.

What did happen: I plucked up that napkin and wiped hard, then balled that thing right up. Planted its lipstick-sullied whiteness on the table in front of me. A flag not of surrender, but of done and done—I really could be, I thought, thinking of my story. I very well could. Once off duty from the conference and class visit and launch, I would traverse the city solo and then sit in my hotel room and sketch ideas. Uncover an ending. Choose the self-erasure of work, my work, over the by now worn out, less salubrious kinds.

Time to leave. The conference organizer settled the bill, the translator withdrew his hand, and we highly acclaimed and good-enoughs rose as if one from the table and gathered ourselves for the afternoon seminars that would precede the rest of the day's packed agenda.

I confess, I did sit in on the translator's. Just in case. Might I not rally, for better or for worse change my mind? I might. I'd known it to happen.

And so I perched on my classroom seat in a state of mild hopefulness, beset by a tepid curiosity as to whether or not I would come to a different decision. And listened as the translator urged the fresh-faced kids to recognize that if they struggled in their work, as they admitted during his session that they had in translating mine, it was most likely the writer's fault.

He paused his pontificating to stare meaningfully at the back row. He shook his head and smirked when the kids turned in concert to see what he was looking at. Clued in, they clenched their jaws and glared accusingly at me. As if betrayed, their innocence robbed.

After all, the translator went on to say, raising his voice, and then pausing again to ensure the return to him of the students' rapt gazes.

Next, a slight bow of the head. A theatrical clearing of the throat.

After all, what's a translator to do? he continued. Translation is at root about movement. One language, one space, shifts to another. Transformation, migration. And so, what can one do with a story in which nothing happens except for someone opening and closing a fridge door?

Which action he pantomimed for the amusement of the tittering students, fingers pressed to their more youthful, less experienced lips.

°

I pace in my hotel room, toss and turn on the bed. No sleep for the wicked. I check the socials on my phone. The room darkens and I gloom-refuse to rouse and turn on a light. Outside, the evening's *passeggiata* begins—through my open window, shoes clack, children laugh. What sounds like a ball wallops across the road. I backhand a few smacks against the carved headboard.

The fuck?

What I've got so far: the man who licked my toes, the woman who sang *this little light of mine* beside me in bed. Both dead now. Also in this story, I've got the osteophytes, dysphagia. Occasional vertigo with its inner-ear woo-woo. I've got the browsing, common misfortunes, such as the mildly enlarged heart. Mother dead. Father might as well be.

Not like you, I'm forced to add in, given today's surprise encounter. Your evergreen scorn, for reasons and treasons real and imagined.

I curl my fingers into claws. Stone breath. An old, rotted wind deep in my bowels.

A tall order to transform this. To migrate this fury over histories not merely mine. The story of you. Story of your sis.

I cramp, too human, stretch, and reach again for my phone. I try my much-reduced father at the nursing home, hoping to prove at least one past has passed.

It's post-lunch there. An aide picks up and says my father's wife isn't around. Busy ripping someone a new one, I surmise, for sending my father's good sweater through the washer-dryer. Or for neglecting to position him strapped into his high-chair-like contraption by the nurse's station for much-needed supervision. Otherwise, my father tries to roam—in a pale version of his former running around, as my mother used to call his power-flirting and cheating—only to hurt himself in disastrous falls.

My father. A lost and once dangerous and maybe still dangerous soul, clambering from his nursing home bed many a wee hour—his sorry state worse at night—to roam the hallways. He dips into other patients' rooms and lifts their bedsheets, an act that potentially visits terror upon them, this is his thing. Until he face-plants on the floor and can't get up. Lies groaning until one of the night staff or someone on the morning shift finds him and determines whether he's injured enough that he needs to go the hospital. Needs at least those needs met.

But it's still daytime there. At my request the aide puts my father on speakerphone. The old guy is mostly silent aside from lip smacks that make me want to tear my hair, and word-like entities I can't make out.

In the background, a TV on, the news, weather. As if from a greater distance, another room, a woman—another inmate, I've heard her before, with her precise, immaculate enunciation—saying, I love you, I love you, I love you.

°

Know I am long divorced. Mostly fiscally and soulfully self-sufficient due to hard and mostly fulfilling academic and creative work—mostly creative, having years ago jumped tracks, lucky me. Hardly desperate at this point in life.

And so, electric with fatigue, and yet unable to sleep, I allow that I'm famished, starving, curious, fine—enough to shower, bandage my ransacked heels, re-dress myself, and head out.

And for fuck's sake, run smack into the French translator, leaning against a pillar in the hotel lobby, checking his screen.

I duck past, and stride into the mild, moist night.

And damned if he isn't beside me as I cross the *campo*. Off the bat, small-talking my ear off—his English excellent, and my Italian next to non-existent, and my French barely that of a semi-bright child. So for certain he has this language thing over me.

In no time he seats himself across from me at the trattoria to which he's ushered us. A hate-date it is. What's in it for him I can guess: the pleasures of asserting, demeaning. But in my defense, I need to eat. Right? To not think, not speak. Coast, and maybe scope out a few shiny, dirty things I might steal off with, bump up the volume on, and layer into a scene or two. Make of myself a spy, an interstellar visitor lurking among the more laughable human specimens.

Also: is he really so bad?

Am I?

We eat, drink. Ageless-seeming men and women with tiny, leashed dogs stroll by. Teens parade, arms linked. Dishware clinks. Canal waves wash beneath a night sky that softens to a sumptuous, starless felt. The server rounds by to ask about dessert. My guy expresses distaste and dismisses the offer, and the server moves on to other customers.

Then my date widens his eyes at me. Oh! he says, a mock polite salted with sarcasm, and a subtle outlining with his hands of my figure. Pardon me, my mistake. You go ahead. *In-dulge.*

My not-covert-enough inattention has cost me. We must draw the line at *dolce*.

I confess: I snicker. He sighs and metes out the last of the red and replaces the bottle on the table with an exaggerated flourish. A pause. Oh, his pauses! I can barely keep from mimicking him—it's true that, given my sleep-deprived state, I've had plenty to drink.

Your problem, he says to the air above me. You use too many words.

The greased shine on his brow. The leg finagled between mine as of ten minutes ago. Oddly glabrous vee of skin where the top of his shirt is unbuttoned. I could also fold in some bulging, comic-sized peepers—but who would buy such a caricature? Who would give a shit? Low-hanging fruit, I decide.

He's not finished though.

C'est une situation grave.

I smile politely, as I had at lunch yesterday, upon encountering his moist, spidery fingers on my knee.

That's it? I say mildly. That's my grave situation?

He makes a putt-putt sound, that's all. Even so, I wish I possessed the witchery of putting him on permanent mute. Erasing him from this moment, yanking him from my head.

Outside my head, into the night air between us—aiming for imperturbable, for cool as an old cunt—I brandish only my held tongue.

°

Didn't my father used to say?

Pointing at me, his little girlfriend. An early reader, bright as can be—bright enough. Possessing enough smarts and natural talent to, with little prompting, sometimes say a thing or two, whatever was on my mind. My father would chuckle with delight at this creature he had made. He'd stoop to tickle my tummy, my whatever he could reach—the man was all sticky fingers throughout my childhood and adolescence, until I bolted the family environs for good, the end, at eighteen—while my emotionally beaten-down, mentally volatile mother, long steeped in a heady brew of violent rage with a milky slash of occasionally doting servility, cringed and wanly stamped her feet at him.

Stop, stop, she'd bleat.

He would not stop. He would boop me with his finger in my private places. A funny game, look how much fun. Or whatever he was thinking. If he was thinking at all, and not simply stuffing his own ruinous version of emotional cotton candy in a space long vacated, or never occupied, within himself. He'd waggle his fingers over my lips, and with evident pride say, Look at all those words coming out of that little mouth!

And to this day—from one day or month or year to the next, however long it takes, wait for it—I *can* be all, hell yeah, get a load of miracle me.

°

I ditch the whack job before the bill arrives. Let him sneer about the bitch he can't fuck.

Solo again, I hustle past luxury shops, clots of crowds with their bursts of languages known and exhilaratingly unknown to me. Footbridges curve like wisps of fog, feral cats circle the outdoor tables of identical-seeming trattorias, antique wood-panelled boats ply the fetid canals—the Venetian brand draping itself before me in its decaying, funland fineries.

Scenes from a movie flicker against church facades: *Don't Look Now*. I pump my limbs, and Donald Sutherland dashes down the mad, snaking passageways after Julie Christie. In the end, he never catches her, she's taken by fiendish trance to a chillier, stranger realm—salve for her grief over the recent death of their child. That was some movie, wasn't it? That sex scene, for one thing. Rumoured to be the real deal, not acted. *Real* real. I remember we three, you and your sister and I, watched the scene together—excuse me, I mean the whole movie—when she and I were fourteen. I remember wondering, is this how life could be? A thing sleek and soigné, a surface gloss over the bullshits life might fling. A series of impeccable glamour shots.

More right turns, a left and left. I'm hoping I won't run into anyone else from the conference. Infinitely preferable, an infinity of strangers. I plow onward, unending rights and lefts and lefts, and my legs turn to paste, I can't catch my breath. For the life of me I can't figure where the fuck I am.

Until, across the canal, the lights from the Lido scribble over the dark water. I know exactly where I am.

At the *fondamenta*, you again. Like me, also gripping the railing. Motionless except for the long black coat you're wearing, even though it's a warm night. The coat lifts in the breeze, fanning like a cape, and you appear to swirl in place.

Slowly, with the utmost stealth, I make my move.

TO B

Fast-forward a decade, give or take, cue up the cue cards again. I'm on a plane flying low over the northern coast of England and across the Irish Sea when I spy Ireland's Eye. A guidebook, pages foxed, lies in my lap. The ancient Poulnabrone Dolmen. The Ardgroom Stone Circle. The oft-plundered monastic site of Clonmacnoise, near the River Shannon, where I might catch sight of the Sheela Na Gig on the carved stonework of the tiny Nun's Church, the real-life women periodically raped and tortured during Viking raids, fun times.

The plane's landing gear engages under me, and more you roars back.

To catch you up: I've been fired. Another first. Like my years-ago trip to Venice, my childhood crush on you. And our shared birth status—I too have a younger sibling, in my case a brother, did you notice I'd so far withheld most mention of him? But yes, fired. I'd been booked to teach a week-long residency course in Dublin, but two months ago my dean pulled my plug. Something about budgets and enrollments from years before I was even on the job. The ruinous cost of thesis advisers with superior expertise, compared to people the dean claimed she could just pull off the street, and our near-screaming matches over such heinous notions. My increasing the-fucks? until I had no fucks left to give. But I'd already forked out for my flight, charging it to my personal credit card before dutifully submitting the receipt and filled-out reimbursement form to finance, so the school felt morally obligated to cover it.

Oh, morals! I unbuckle my seat belt, rise to the scrum surrounding the overhead bins, and wonder whether to feel pissed or sad about lost opportunities. Or—as carry-ons pell-mell around me and I duck to avoid decapitation, bladder a hornet's nest—whether to feel elated. Thrilled at now wheeling my luggage through the jetport, searching out the closest bathroom, visions of a full Irish breakfast and ale at some quaint pub dancing in my head.

I decide: elated. Oh, the perfidy! Of making off with something to which I no longer have any right.

°

On the outskirts of Dublin Airport, I rent a car. From there I make the rounds, eat the cheese, drink the beer. Try to forget stuff. Try to catch some sleep. Not sleeping: to this day, another one of my things.

And so, two days into my trip and still jet-lagged, manoeuvring the twisty Ring of Kerry—frantically trying to recall the right from the wrong side of the road, my toy-sized rental tucked between juggernaut tour buses—I nearly miss a cliff-side turn. On my third day I get lost navigating the desert-like Burren, with its mazes of tall, spiny hedges lining narrow roads with few intersections, just bends, bending for hours until I feel I might break—until I pop out exactly where I'd wanted to be, surprised as an inept mole. That night, at the local in the village where I'm staying, I rewatch a Tom Cruise vehicle where he's running for all he's worth, hands chopping the air, as he does. I get a few pints in, weary-shaky from the misadventures of my past few days. Tired sick—or just plain bored—from what feels like my lifetime thus far of misadventures. How I too could go and go, no matter my travails or bad decisions. Until, at some point I can't yet see, I don't.

Bored, I decide, and settle my bill.

°

The next morning I throw it in, arrange to ditch the rental. Things could suck worse than spending the rest of my trip submitting to group tours. And then, my second-last day, things do suck worse. I really am sick. On the tour van. Upchucking into my daypack, while the other tourists huddle in the wind on a mountaintop, near the set of an apparently popular TV show about fourth-century invaders.

You again. I wipe my face with a crumpled tissue dug from an outer, unbreached pocket of my bag, and wonder what you might have on tap concerning this pseudo-site. Some *bon mots* based on the unassailable archaeological record. Or simply the snide snort I remember too well—your kid sister and I too clownish, too dull, too *too* for your esteemed company, which we nevertheless ecstatically craved.

That night, the next morning, I'm unable to keep food or liquid down. In my costly, cramped Dublin apartment rental I unscrew my head and set it in the shower, where it sings and talks to itself. The rest of me lies gasping on the pleather couch until I pass out. I come to in the darkest pre-dawn, clammily clutching my tablet.

In a delirium I do the deed: search for your faculty email address. A cinch to find.

And then fuck the email, I go straight to message on your office phone.

Hello? Hello? Thanks for your order, just calling to confirm. How many pieces of chicken? Sweet and sour, or extra-spicy hot?

◦

What I've slunk off with, made much of, outright thieved.

That old story? The one I honestly, maybe honestly, thought you'd never in a million read. An old, borrowed tale. Long before Venice, I switched it around and dressed it up, but basically: Osiris marries sister Isis, gets offed and dismembered by jealous brother, body parts scattered to the four winds. Isis incarnates as a kite—that pocket-sized, aerobatic raptor with laser-keen eyesight. Soars and swoops, recovers brother-husband bits. Stitches them together, to enable his journey whole to the underworld, and the possibility of resurrecting him. Transformation, migration, it's all there. Despite what that jerk of a translator once claimed. My work done, if not exceedingly well.

I know: Egyptology's not your field. But the pages turn anyway, who can keep track? I couldn't. Still can't.

In my version, who but me stands in for the jealous brother, jealous at being set aside? When I think about you two: that close.

The part of me that stands in, too, for the kite: the small raptor who threads the parts, commits the long con of tying the pieces together.

Maybe you had read it.

Might account for the laugh you spat at our Venetian meet-uncute. Sparking me to flee the *fondamenta* and next morning the magnificent, maddening city. And by the time I touched down at Dulles, my hopes for this very story. Yarn of a yarn whose pieces I couldn't and still can't lash together, as I can't resurrect the dead in their kingdom of the past. Our shared past. The three we once were together—you, your sister, and I—now dead to me. This story I still can't get to end.

°

Thirty-seven hours later, a decade post-Venice, I'm home from Dublin and still awaiting your reply, pneumonia my companion, in bed a week now, hacking up chunks of sodden lung. Twice this morning my nose has brushed the ceiling, I can't manage beyond a sip of water at a time, wheeze with what feels like the last breaths in the old windbags. I should call someone. A doctor, if I were in my right mind. If I weren't, if I were suffering one of my wrong minds, I'd call my ex-husband. Except he refuses to pick up when he sees his old hon on caller ID. Or I could summon up a neighbour or two. People I nod at on the street and ask to collect my mail the infrequent times I'm gone. Or an ex-colleague semi-friend? Might as well summon the long-dead family dog.

I could call my kid brother. Remember him? Except this isn't that story. It's mine and yours, a picaresque that ends, so far, with me pretty much fucked.

°

Eventually my fever breaks, and I'm well enough to make weak tea and watery broths—as a point of principle, though, I refuse the fridge door. I sit bundled in layers of saggy sweaters on my front porch for long, derelict hours, watch fall leaves snicker onto the sidewalk. At first frost I take to the couch, where the last leaves drift in my head. Daily I sharpen my hearing on the local late-year crickets, giant-legged and black as coal, hopping my floors. Job, what job? Savings? I can assure you, not.

The year ends, the end of the crappy year. Fireworks. Applause. My couch, and me on it, hugging my laptop, livestreaming, deep digging the search engines, dropping the ball, contemplating picking it up—better believe, do I ever have my laptop.

So don't you worry, I'm still ticking, I'm good, creeping ever on. Creep-writing you again. Or is it that I'm writing me?

°

Herself let it drop. Tiger-eye eyes, gold and brown, but her words blithe as a songbird, flitting from this subject to that: her next semester's courses, new pair of shiny boots, part-time job at a bookstore, new pals she'd made and how fucking fascinating they were, tra fucking la. The greatness of this actor guy she used to fuck. And how could I not have known about you and her? This one-sided convo taking place the last time I ever saw her. Could stand to see her. At a by now long non-existent cheesy joint with checkered tablecloths. A litre of shitty white wine set out before us, not even cold.

°

I stop wondering why I can't assign blame, or who to assign it to. I recover, rustle up freelance work, part-time gigs. Make the ends sort of meet. The past continues its past life without me.

Sometimes I take out my old notes and apprise them like the droppings of an oracle I can't quite read. Unable to find the plot points. Make things happen.

Not much happens.

Until COVID hits, the border closes, my father's wife dies. My father—he's held on this long, some kind of miracle man—further declines, it's bad, he's bad. My poor kid brother holds down the fort, but still. When the border reopens, provisionally, lots of red tape to cut through, I drive north for two days and customs waves me through—family emergency, hop to it. But first I see a few old acquaintances in the city to which our childhood suburb clung. I pace the much-altered, billionaire-colonized streets. And three days pass before I continue farther north, past the terroir of our youth, and enter the zone of luxury townhouse developments and mega-house compounds where once lay calming, crop-less fields.

I do it: succeed in locating the nursing home, in which I undertake the rapid test and pass go. And then, secretly wishing I'd not passed—or that I could request a redo, an un-pass—I ascend in the elevator to the memory ward. I've never before visited and am happy to confirm my brother's impression that the place looks clean, the staff professionally upbeat. I find the old guy in the common room, parked in his special wheelchair in front of a giant screen showing a Hallmark movie from maybe thirty years ago. Not that he pays it any attention. Nor does he heed my tap on his shoulder.

Against the rules, but just trying to help the old fiend out, I pull my mask down. That gets him. He peers. Lifts his wiry brows, soundlessly works his mouth. He is ninety-seven. Gripped by late-stage dementia. Hemoglobin dangerously low, he's too old to keep transfusing him. Finally, he's in end-of-life care.

Even so—looked at another way, especially so—I can tell what's coming. Sort of. Something that's my fault. He is my fault. His moods, unhappiness, anger at my betrayals, my rejecting him—all on me.

NO, he suddenly roars. I. CAN'T. GO.

Izzy! a nurse calls out.

My father slumps forward, presses his face to the plastic tray attached to the front of his wheelchair—the most abject gesture of despair I have ever seen.

I manage to sort of make good. Rub his frail back, murmur what I hope are comforting sounds. What I think a decent person might decently do in the situation.

He springs upright again—surprise! His face crimson now, pouched in on itself. The look of fury that terrified me as a kid. Scrambled me sideways to the bathroom to lodge myself between the shut door and toilet to prevent him from busting in and taking his belt to his little girlfriend. His well-starred first born. She who'd rejected his wink or tickle or crude comment, thwarted him, gone so far as to scoff, or dare to take her life in her hands and shrug him off.

He is a suffering of skin and bones now, but before I can in all decency self-correct, I take a giant step back.

SHIT, he roars. FUCK.

Izzy! a different nurse calls. No swears!

That quiets him. The other patients continue to stare at the large screen at the front of the room—a soundless sequence in black and white, two characters tapping out a dance sequence in a juke joint—or gaze at their own mostly immobilized feet. One patient, surprisingly youthful looking, I peg him as early fifties, stands up, sits down, ups and downs. I listen for the woman I've overheard on the phone saying, I love you, I love you—but I have no idea what she looks like, I don't hear her now, maybe gone for good. Onscreen, a kiss shapes up.

These nurses—they've seen it all, I bet. I sense them taking me in, spitting me out. Double cringe: Daddy's one-time star, and a point of interest these women sharpen their gaze on.

Options, please!

Step up, assume the sentimental position, possibly for the last time stroke my father's age-swollen fingers, pat his lovelorn back, hug him, mumble a few words. Or bail fast, hightail it before the corny, sham resolution cranks into view.

Either version a radioactive effigy with a forever half-life. Unforgettable until I forget it all away.

My father speaks up again, saying it for me: SHIT. FUCK.

This time the nurses don't intervene.

I decide to give it five more minutes.

Can you believe? I take ten.

AND BACK AGAIN

If you're thinking this is one of those stories that go nowhere, where you don't know where this is going—where I don't know—rest assured, I've got this, the old head really is on straight. The lot of we first borns: we lead the way though our mistakes be legion, marked from birth for such sacrifice. In this spirit, I come to you now, having learned from online sources of your sudden proximity: the lecture you're to deliver tonight in support of your latest book, a guide to archaeology for the generalist. The event is at one of this nation's more venerable institutions, ripe with the wonders and plunders of the ages, good on you. On us both, as we're both approaching our senior years, and I dress with care, a smart wool coat and oversized, tasteful scarf, wanting you to see I've once again come up in the world, I've landed on my feet. On the metro I check my reflection in the window opposite me: upright posture, check. At my stop I ascend the steep escalator, reviewing the details of my plan, and soon enough take a seat in the hall, second row on the right. I'm early, plenty of time to reconsider and hoof it out the door, but then I spy you, up front on the left, chatting with the likely director of programming, and the journalist who'll interview you onstage once you've talked your talk.

This is where I'm going, I think. Where I've arrived. This night, this place, gold-painted seats arrayed under a ceiling mural of angels and trumpets. I can hardly believe it—the years, the effort.

Don't you look nice, too. Pressed pants and shirt. Fusty tweed vest, rambling grey beard. They help you look the part.

The event begins. You speak into the microphone at the podium. I tilt my damned head, stroke finger against chin, relish my part, as if hanging on your every hyper-articulated word. Most of which I don't take in, but never mind, I'm here for you. Me in my chicken suit and the sky is falling, I've dropped in on you, straight through the ceiling mural and past the angels and trumpets, straight from the falling sky. I've arrived, as I've said, second row on the right.

Your talk and interview over, I queue in the bookseller's line and then in the line to have you sign my purchase, my polite request to have you address it to me locked and loaded in my mouth. I've brought my best pen. I've brought an exchange too: an offering. It's tucked in my bag. A compendium, swell of details, crisscrossing uncertainties—I'm convinced it's my best work.

My turn. But on my final approach, your confused alarm disarms me—you must recognize my face, I hadn't counted on that—and I chase the words in my throat until I get the general idea out, my name. You pull off a curt nod, and I pull my pages from my bag, and you grudgingly accept my gift. This Henny Penny smash-up I've already signed. For you.

I thank you for coming. I say I enjoyed your talk.

What just happened? your face says, then you swiftly look behind me for whoever is next.

I should've known a drink would be out of the question.

°

We're at a movie. A long one. Kurosawa, if I remember correctly. You and teenaged me and your sister. She who in the end would never move from our childhood neighbourhood, a place gussied up in recent years, but mostly the same old. So much for her adolescent claims of future glory directing films and plays. She who once directed herself in the starring role of her life, and ours. I've saved this for the end, reluctant to speak ill of the dead. Since in the end, she upped and died too young, a first at least in that. And remained a star, a dark inferno, in my life. And yours? Given everything. But before her death and this continuing aftermath, before her casual revelation of the secret past between you and her, this screening. We're in New York—New York!—on a trip organized by your undergraduate art history class, a trip on which your sister and I, fan-girling our asses off over you, have managed to talk our way into coming with. My first time in notorious mid-seventies New York. A time we—but here the memory death-rattles in a flapping off the old reel and ends.

°

Same trip. A roaring snow in Central Park pixelates us into oblivion, the paradox of a preserved eclipse. Is this how things end? Your sister, my best friend, twirling in her ankle-length, thrifted black velvet coat. Her own gravitational center. Her starlet flash amid the thick flakes that spotlight her doom drama: her grand hopes for the future already salted away—she must have known even then that she could never be the leading lady. Not with the cruel and limiting expectations of those times. Not with her stocky build similar to yours, nor with her perfectly sturdy thighs she bared to the public eye only on summer days at the cottage your grandfather built, beach sand turning our ill-fitting bikinis to gold dust. Otherwise, she never wore pants, never shorts, only sweeping dresses and flaring outerwear that artfully concealed her shape. Another paradox: she had already understood, in her self-loathing, that she would need to direct, accept the god role. On this afternoon in Central Park, one last twirl, one last dissolve to black of her dreams, while the zoo's bison and bears blink like giant backdrop, and you and I keep the hell out of the frame. You too cool in your round wire-rims and peacoat. Me in a drab green parka making drab exclamations about my friend, resigned to egging her on, encouraging her vertiginous, centre-stage performance. You and I reduced to beasts of burden, shouldering the baffling, burdensome loves we feel for her.

°

More fragments. Early strata. Her fastidiously groomed pussy, Bonne Bell lip blush coating her erect nipples. Those high school afternoons, my desperation. Her green bedroom walls. The tequila shots she plies me with so I can bust through the ceiling and take myself out for a float around the nearby park, the ceiling that wafts to greater heights on her spritzes of Je Reviens by Worth eau de toilette, with its middle notes of narcissus, heights hard to reach. Nips from her sharp teeth leave bruises on my baby-fat belly.

Other afternoons, watching her act a scene in high school theatre class—she's too violent, too burdened, bursting to let loose some shattering revelation. Her pretty summer dresses to match the blue satin ribbons wound around her ankles, the effortful impression of feminine delicacy to belie the aggressive roar within, the powerful build—so afraid is she of appearing butch. The actor friend in high school who she fucks in secret, an experience she regales only me with, given the need to keep his official girlfriend in the dark, in a dark game of snakes and ladders, who's up, who's down. Given the need for an audience, and I'm at hand, the one to applaud as she bursts into flame. The one to behold her strange, hot heart. Heart so original, I believe back then. Need to believe, to elevate myself. Feel lapped in possibility. Needing the promise—more fantasy, as it turned out, than real—of a more frictionless place than my bitter-tasting, carcinogenic home life.

Musk of her soiled underwear as laundry day approaches—your house equipped with neither a working washer nor dryer. Your car-less, single mother needing a once-weekly drive from a neighbour to the laundromat—a neighbour with extramarital interests in your mother, a man your exhausted mother must both entertain and keep at arm's length.

C'est incroyable! Je n'en reviens pas. Reviens, chérie.

More pieces of you. You strut through the downtown Toronto crowds in the same peacoat, after a different movie, with your mother, sister, and me. Your chin thrust forward, breathing contempt for hockey fans and fast food, more things to feel superior to. Your attempts at painting, and the canvas you enter in a competition, a self-portrait: half your shocked face, the other half dirt, a substrate yielding rock, bones, a fork and spoon, an empty pot. Your grin, pleased with your magnanimity, when one Christmas morning I'm thrilled to unwrap the paperback copy of *Sir Gawain and the Green Knight* you deign to educate me with. Oh, courtly tales!

°

More chips off the old block, but trust me, we're finally getting somewhere. On the trip to New York, there's the Chinatown dinner at which a handsome grad student joins us. He's even more impressively older than you and, as we're getting up to leave, he reaches across our rusted cups of tea to slip his hand on mine. A pass. My first, my very own, a thing distinct from the tripwires your sister lays for me. I startle, jerk back my hand—a moment forever arrested in my head. I cluelessly wait the rest of the weekend for him to approach me again. Never happens. But it's something, a start, I hope. But with no clue how to scratch the surface of these freeze-frames. To compass their extravagant detail. Detail that accumulates like the weight these too many words can't hold. Words trying to figure if we three together, or in pairs or singles, were lucky to have loved. Or were doomed by our love. Or—maybe I still can't see it, rock bottom, the end.

°

Noon, our last day in New York. We're in a slice shop. I've missed the lead-up signs, but suddenly you two need to have words, urgent ones you both deem I'm not allowed to overhear.

Go entertain yourself for awhile, one of you says, lips a coiled smile.

Think you can manage that? the other chimes in.

A lover's spat. I should have known. Sort of did know? At the time?

Oh, Oracle. All this dirt. Some of it not even mine.

For my portion—banished. My status rendered clear: I'm the third wheel in the story of you and your sister.

My first more-than inkling, though it would take years for the truth to punch me so hard in the face I'd never be able to forget, forgive, dream it away.

At noon that day, I take to the New York sidewalk. Humiliated, exiled, sick at heart. The easily dismissed friend, your sister's play-sex practice cunt, weak competitor. But did you never regard me as competition too? Never? I plod alone, quickly lost. A snaggle-toothed, sticky snow freezes my cheeks and gums my lashes.

Icy blocks of this, before they turn to fuck this.

I clamber aboard a city bus and ride stops I disdain to count. Get off who knows where and find a store selling cheap souvenirs, in which I purchase a crappy ashtray I'll gift my younger brother—the memory of which pains me to this day, for all the reasons. Purchase in hand, I again pound the pavement. No idea where I am in the mounting slush. I wonder if I've been away long enough. If it's safe to return. I doubt I can even find my way back to the hotel, back on time—our chartered bus leaves at four o'clock on the dot, we were warned, be there or, basically, be screwed. No nighttime border crossing, no passport check. No home.

Remember home?

Skyscrapers tower above me like totems, fierce and blank, jabbing the blank sky. I halt, stamp footprints in tiny circles to warm my toes. The glass-and-stone structures yaw, rotate a notch, then another. Crystals inside a watch. Star-eyed snowflakes. The constellations of crystals in my inner ear shifting—a spinning, summoning vertigo gyring me deeper inside something, a somewhere else inside me. Proper adults race past muttering, elbowing, annoyed that some dumb kid blocks their path.

I decide: time. I gather myself as if in my own arms and descend a set of wet stairs that lead to the roaring, rushing subway.

I leave you here, with this version of me. Soon to be solitary among the crowds. Soon to pick my way among them and pay my fare like a pro, and enter the underworld's windy, rushing spaces, humid as mouths. My mind blessedly empty, cavernous as I approach the platform and glean the begrimed tracks and rot-bruised wind. My blood in clots like snarls of ill-used words—those of the wizened god I've grown inside me. Head a halo of cunning stitches of rodent tails and tale snippets. Heart a box of broken glass, a nostalgia of shards for which later, much later, I might, through hard work and great luck, find use.

Behold me if you dare, this god might say, in a language new to me—fresh to me even now, all these years later.

If she wanted to say. If she felt like it. Moved by what ancient convulsions. What savage, caustic silences.

I'm not there yet. But if memory serves me right, soon I'll descend another set of steps. A great rattle will announce itself. An endless line of cars will appear, each replete with sleeping strangers, myself welcomed among them.

The question all along: not where to end, but where to begin.

Stair railing in hand, on my way to somewhere else, I held on tight.

Once Then Suddenly Later

We vent the hot gas, yet remain semi-aloft, at the mercy of the rising wind. The gondola tips sideways, and we swerve low over fields, swooping so near telegraph wires we hear the gale strop the lines. We avoid decapitation by a hair.

°

When I say *we* I refer to my older brother and myself. Louis and Jules Godard, also brothers, who designed our monster, the world's largest aerostat. Their assistant Gabriel Yon. And the other passengers, all of them inexperienced aeronauts, including the Princesse de La Tour d'Auvergne, slight of build and elegantly attired.

A complement of thirteen: the number my brother has, in a show of anti-superstition bravado, alighted upon and made most public.

°

Le Géant. First flight. Sunday, October 4, 1885. Two hundred thousand Parisians pay one franc apiece to line the parade ground of Champ de Mars. A mixed success. My brother believed twice as many would come.

°

Witness the double envelopes—sewn from twenty-two thousand yards of silk—slowly inflate, and bell two stories high.

According to enthralled reports, one could see it from anywhere in the capital.

°

Tethers released, our craft sails above the city on a gentle breeze. For three hours we venture forth over France. The world below, a quilt of creation. Under a skim of clouds we dine and drink champagne in the two-level wicker cabin replete with kitchen and lavatory, printing press, darkroom, wine cellar, bunk beds, our fascinating crowd—my brother hopes we will fly all the way to Russia. At dusk, we race above the velvet blanket of ground, beneath an empurpled sky. We light lanterns, and the *princesse* offers a smile when I refill her glass. I carve the roast venison, reserving the most succulent morsels for her plate. Post-sup, I anchor myself to her side, and when our giant sways, my shoulder touches hers. *Princesse, pardonnez-moi!* Her laugh rings, but she refuses me small talk. But what is talk when elation buoys my breast? When I dare hope to search out hers, round and firm, outlined through her fashionable garments.

°

Night comes and we lose our bearings. The wind shouts. Rain falls. The Godards and Yon confer, tug ropes. The balloon shrinks, the gondola shudders, and the *princesse* clasps my arm, her nails bite through my coat. Spirit emboldened fuses to flesh, and we too are writ vast, proof of the existence of human gods.

It is nothing, nothing at all, my brother blusters, as the jerks of the gondola and shrieks of the passengers mount.

I could not agree and disagree with him more, were I able to speak.

Fear not, he bellows.

The cabin crunches ground, bucks into the air. Dragged onward by the deflating silks, our boat is a delirium of dear lords and oh shits and mad barking cries. In the commotion, my brother—my older and illustrious, red-haired brother—knocks me from my feet, and the *princesse* forfeits her grip on my sleeve.

°

We careen miles over the countryside, cabin bashing into treetops.

We swing lower, terrifying the sheep and cows from their sheep and cow dreams, their bawls and bleats a wild uproar.

We plow into telegraph wires that by a fraction fail to guillotine us, we tear out the telegraph poles. They finick behind us like fangs.

I too can spark pictures in the mind.

My celebrated brother—illustrator, devastating political caricaturist, sought-after photographer of Bernhardt and Dumas *père et fils*, Sand with her lively bonnets, Baudelaire, and Hugo, the tender lion—is not the only gifted one.

My brother the vigorous anti-royalist. Fiery seeker and dazzling inventor, haughty minion of reason and progress. Modernity's seer, the future will conceivably claim—I can see it now, clinging for dear life in the bucking gondola, know that I too have the knack of foresight, my brother is not alone in this.

This brother larger than life reeks like a goat in rut, though he has no truck with any barnyard.

My brother like a beast with hot coals for eyes.

°

In the nighttime murk, the Godards and Yon shed more ballast. Once more safely aloft, we yet cower. What of our descent? We cannot humanly remain airborne forever.

Out of her element, the *princesse* clings tight as a barnacle to my brother's neck.

I—who am not so atremble, bowels quaking, that I no longer possess two eyes in my own head—sink to my shins with a croak.

°

When we crash for good—in a rain-drenched field twenty-five miles east of Paris, near Meaux— by some miracle dubious or stupefying, my twisted knee is the sole injury sustained by those aboard.

°

In this photograph, taken by no one two weeks later, I stand to attention at Champ de Mars, as much as my lame leg allows.

Also in attendance to witness *The Giant*'s second launch: Emperor Napoléon III and the young king of Greece, though my brother the staunch republican seems not to care. He sequesters in the service hut next to the balloon, emerging only to greet the royals with the declaration, *Je suis M. Nadar!* and bruit a few notions concerning aerial navigation, before clambering his clownishly long legs aboard for the cast off. *Bon voyage, M. Nadar!*

There are nine passengers in total for this escapade, the polypheme's second. Most are more experienced than on the previous undertaking.

Nearly all: my brother has convinced his wife, Ernestine, to join him.

Beloved Ernestine. She is plain of face, as in this portrait, taken two years earlier by my brother at the studio at 11, Rue des Capucines—a studio once mine. But make no mistake. She possesses a scrupulous mind. She keeps my brother's accounts, and mine. Once a month she invites me to family tea.

°

Yesterday I limped uninvited to her door, knowing my brother spent these hours racing from office to café to drawing room. Hounding for publicity, baying for more funds to secure ever more publicity, nosing intemperately toward fresh fame.

She receives me. She pours and passes our cups and saucers. I breathe in the steam, nerves thrumming. We are seated side by side on the divan in her parlour. The green velvet curtains are drawn, and a fire snaps its irregular music from the fireplace. Otherwise, silence. Her level gaze unnerves me. She settles her teacup and saucer on the side table and raises a dish of sugared almonds.

She will break my heart. One day her cool kindness will train too taut the pulleys in my chest, until they screech, and I tumble broken to the ground.

Then I remember: I must break myself, for her sake I must burst the seams of my circumspection and warn her.

I suppress a cough. I lick my lips. My dear Ernestine, I say, voice strangely high. Permit me a word.

The dish remains level with my head, which pounds. What runs through the veins of this woman, unflappable as stone? The blood cannot be the same as what knuckles through mine.

My voice drones sour and thin, in view of my brother's latest enterprise, the dangers pursuant. My brother the flamboyant contrarian, seeking to prove the necessity of heavier-than-air flight—by promoting a huge balloon doomed to fail. As a woman of superior intelligence, surely she also knows the reasons my brother gives for his zealotry: flight generated by an engine can be controlled, whereas a balloon is too passive, blown here and there by the fickle winds. Of course she understands. Does she also realize that my brother seeks to heighten the spectacle by carting his precious wife along for the ride? Yes? Is she also aware that my brother, with his fiend's ambition, cares less for her safety than for his renown?

This last is not my first lie. Or is it not a lie? My mind wavers and drifts. The clock on the mantel ticks, and Ernestine trains her plain face on me, and I freeze to find I have been in motion, my fallible feet are not where I had planted them on the floor. A twitch overtakes my cheek. Ernestine gives the dish a mild shake, and the almonds clink.

In truth, under Ernestine's unblemished gaze, I cannot tell which way the truth lies.

I have spilled tea on my trousers. Chastened, I recall a small slice of my manners and shake my head.

She tilts hers. No? Mercifully, no smile, however faint, flickers from her. No sign, either, of assent to, or judgment of, the suit I have placed before her.

In truth, lack of judgment of me remains one of Ernestine's strong, if not confounding, traits.

If I were my older and flaming torch of a vainglorious brother, a roar would sear my throat, and sally forth to disavow and forswear and repudiate and refuse. To say, *No chance,* to a comet of a brother such as mine. I would arise to pace the patterned rug and strike the silly, flowery dish from her hand. I would urge my own fire to brazen forth.

I neglect to stand and shout. My musing shocks only myself. It remains in my head as a congenital smoulder, except for what tricks forth a minute movement in my arm, which of its own accord sweeps out and brushes hers.

She shifts a fraction in the opposite direction and replaces the dish on the side table with a click.

The sound echoes between my temples in radiating flashes. Stupefaction follows. A scarlet tangle of hot thoughts. Like my brother, I too could seek more. Could I not? Hoist my hand along her flank, rustle her dress silks. Induce a lifting, billowing motion.

More tea?

I deploy my hand, woodenly feign stroking my wisps of unsatisfactory beard, and resettle myself on the divan in an unimpeachable position, secure in the extent to which I am shut from intelligence of my brother and his wife's conjugal stratagems, their devotions and plans that remain impenetrable by me.

As if I am brother to myself, an older brother much esteemed by the world and whose younger brother is not—an older brother who takes increasing pleasure, it sometimes strikes me, in putting his younger brother in his place, hectoring, lecturing, ignoring—I recall that I cannot always perceive which way the world outside, and the one inside me, lie in relation to each other. I cannot see if they lie together. If they fit or not.

According to this older brother, as enumerated in his most recent appraisals, I must not undertake determinations based on lies, my lies, that I cannot always tell are lies. Who can? I cannot. I cannot always tell which way the winds of my lies will blow.

I set my half-emptied teacup and saucer on the opposite side table. I hunch my shoulders, sink deeper into the cushions.

For more moments than I care to count, my unfortunate mouth stumbles on in expert mimicry of empty air.

Ernestine's silence is plain as her face. Plainly, tomorrow she will rise over Paris and beyond.

°

The Giant lifts. The crowd gasps, and cries of delight and clapping ring out. From my position on the parade ground, I lift my arm still fizzling from yesterday's infecund contact, and I wave. I search for the plain face, and see only my brother, disinclined to wave back.

In this photograph taken by no one, I cast my backside to the crowd.

I lower my head, brow heavy, hooded eyes downcast, hair a dark, trammelled wave.

My wretched knee aches. I long to sit, lie down.

I lower my suddenly aching arm, and its empty sweep outlines the exact shape of misfortune. I emit a miasma of despondence, of misfit, to the tips of my curled toes.

In the aftermath of yesterday's excitation, I am—as often follows my experiences in the company of women—the very picture of gloom.

Even my tongue drags, as in these sentences bearing the noxious emissions of one cast out. The drench of self-pity.

True to type, I am stranded by my brother's diktat: my disposition deemed a corrupt amplitude, at once too extravagant, and too leaden, for anyone's good.

°

In this one, I am on view for all to see: one for the ages, this photograph by my brother. More proof, should any be required, of his faultless capacity for capturing the essence of his subject's soul.

(*See:* my brother Gaspard-Félix Tournachon, born April 6, 1820. A *fils naturel* on his birth certificate, as our parents are not yet married, faithful to Robespierre's revolutionary ideals. Bastard brother. He dons the mantle of his nickname around 1849. *Je suis* M. *Nadar!* His signature lies emblazoned in red glass tubing by Lumière *père*, and mounted between the third and fourth stories of his final and most luxurious studio at 35, boulevard des Capucines. His pantheon of notables unceasingly trundles in to have their portraits done. Each a study of the individual human countenance, of vital psychological depth through the means of light on paper. An intimacy and closeness obtains between viewer and subject, and simultaneously a distance—a standing away, an apartness—that proposes an assertion, if not an outright invention of, the primacy of selfhood. Each portrait a *Je suis!*)

Accomplished four years before my brother's aerial escapades and undertaken in the previous studio—as I have remarked, a studio once mine—at 11, Rue des Capucines, this portrait of me reveals a countenance of sluggish mien, an embarrassment of facial hair. A failure to blaze hot as my brother's red hair. Already, in this three-quarter view of my face, my brother undermines and mocks me. I dull, my gaze a miscreation: everywhere, and too inward, all at once.

My brother's triumph.

°

In this one, which my brother fails to capture, mountaintop grasses bend under a stiff breeze. My brow is creased and weighted. Pain bristles my knee. I lie down, drink from my flask. Clouds sail. Smell of cow shit. Elsewhere, it is still early in *The Giant*'s second jaunt. My brother's and the passengers' only fear, albeit improbable, is that they might drift over the North Sea.

Later, my brother commissions me to draw the crazed-comet, near-collision with an oncoming train.

I am glad for the money. My work is excellent. My vantage elevated, we encounter a panorama in which we view the deflating balloon and tipped gondola approach the unrelenting engine of progress.

See it wave its menace of black smoke. Trees whip in the gale. In the left foreground, toy-sized horses and sheep race for their lives.

My brother's breathless account of the ordeal, and my epic scene, are published in the best newspapers.

Can it not be argued, who lifts whom?

o

In truth, of which there is also no photograph, on Sunday, October 18, 1863, I am not atop a mountain viewing the triumph and catastrophe of *Le Géant* on its second hop. I am not observing with dispassion, with objective and scientific integrity, as befits our increasingly and elegantly enlightened time. I am not readying to encapsulate the scene in my excellent drawing.

I remain instead in Paris, having left the parade grounds at Champ de Mars to drink in a tavern in Montmartre, newly annexed by the city, while my brother chivalrously clutches Ernestine, his courageous wife—here, I raise my smeared glass—hoping to shield her from harm.

Already he is spinning, spinning his tale.

I spin mine, my brother's brother.

A week later, in the din of another Montmartre tavern, I drain my glass to the dregs. I wipe my mouth on my sleeve. This is the day: my brother's exhortations concerning the right-to-flight for all, and my lie of a drawing, flash into countless outstretched hands. All of Paris is breathless to take in the tale.

In my brother's telling, the fresh disaster ends by the bank of a stream in Germany, from whence the injured—they are all injured, but lucky to be alive—are conducted with alacrity to Hanover, where King George V himself and his loving royal family oversee the crew and passengers' pampered convalescence.

Is my brother not the most fortunate man alive?

In the tavern, my heart hangs naked and dimming in my chest, a dying bulb.

Outside, Paris shapes up on Baron Haussmann's newly planned streets—everyone mad for the flawless, rational approach. The future nears. Any fool can see. My ears whine, and I rap on the table with my empty glass. Another pour, I beg you.

I long for the days of dirt and dishevelment. The jumbled strata of odd angles to the streets mirroring the soul's derelictions. Rafts of the city's phantasms, half living and half dead, whose paroxysms match mine.

I hoist the refill above my head before I drink.

Better Ernestine in my brother's arms than a *princesse*.

To progress, I conclude with a grunt.

∘

Je suis M. Nadar! For the sake of truth, let the record show: this was my first lie. Or rather, misrepresentation: long before *The Giant*'s flights, I filched my brother's increasingly famous name. I, in the first flush of my youth, had failed in my ambitions as a painter. My brother stepped up, and installed me at 11, Rue des Capucines, as any decent older brother would. His idea: photography a recent technology, and wildly popular. I took quickly to the technology, it is I who took those early pictures—and not my brother, already celebrated, notorious for his political illustrations and screeds, the unruly bohemian parties that stoked gossip and admiration and envy of the new. In this second flush of youth, afforded me by my already infamous brother, I was the photographer, the studio mine—it is I who was not above stamping my brother's moniker on the backs of my prints.

In my defence: beside the name, in tiny letters, nested the *jne*.

Yes, I did blur my lie with this bantam truth: I was Nadar the Younger.

But let the record also show: since the *jeune* was greatly diminutive, I shrank.

And yet I ignited my brother's ire. He sued me, I sued him back, we lost our heads, and money bled from us both like shared blood. In this way, at least, we were as one.

Until Ernestine once more invited me to tea.

In the drawing room, pacing before the divan, where Ernestine had seated me, my brother proposed the points to his peace offering.

He would clear my debts, as he remained considerably more financially solvent than I. He would wield his influence to direct a steady stream of less desirable clients to my studio. He would endeavour to secure some kind of position for me in his future projects.

(*See:* I become a passenger for *The Giant*'s first journey. *See:* my drawing, previously viewed, of the episode with the train during the second misadventure.)

At their home, in the drawing room, Ernestine seated next to me on the divan, my brother settled into the upholstered *bergère,* from which he poked the glowing logs in the fireplace. Outside, November, stark with cold.

Do you see, he asked, speaking over his shoulder, that you would have a guaranteed living of sorts?

My eyes prickled: I saw, I understood. My mimicry had set in motion the mechanism by which he would forever put me in my place. Humanity's glorious future eras would ascend without me.

Ernestine with her plain face stirred beside me and poured more tea. She raised a platter of tea cakes.

More? Would I accept?

Plainly, I was no longer young.

°

Following the escapades with *Le Géant*, my brother proceeds to birth aerial reconnaissance.

(*See:* the outbreak of the Franco-Prussian war in 1870, for which he undertakes tethered ascents in smaller balloons, and reports on enemy activities beyond the city.

See: my brother births the world's first airmail service, when poor Paris is encircled—its citizens starving and unable to reach family through telegraph and post, leaders unable to communicate with Tours, where a provisional government sits—when all of poor besieged Paris is prevented from relaying the dire situation to the rest of the world, my brother arranges to stock a balloon with two hundred and fifty pounds of mail.

The silks are leaky, susceptible to Prussian sharpshooters, the Prussians who will execute any *aérostier* as a spy.

A man other than my brother is onboard, a seasoned and brave aeronaut who contrives to fly high enough to avoid Prussian muskets. He lands three hours after lift off, fifty miles west of Paris, and undertakes the rest of the journey to Tours by cart and rail.

On subsequent missions, these balloons ferry caged homing pigeons. Microfilm, invented a decade earlier, enables the photographing and shrinking of return correspondence to Paris. These copies are rolled into goose-quill tubes, and the tubes then attached via waxed silk thread to the tail feathers of the loyal birds.

The creatures are a soft, lactic grey. I bear witness, uselessly stalking Haussmann's perfectly ordered streets of starvation and fear in the ashen wartime light.)

°

The world changes. I change, but not so much. It is my brother who continues to experiment, now with photography via electric refulgence, and so invents underground photography. It is my brother—I cannot keep up—who descends like a hero into Haussmann's new catacombs and sewers to showcase the sanitized future that follows the terrible cholera epidemics.

(*See:* the bones of the dead, dug from their pine beds in local cemeteries, and stacked in organized piles beneath the city. *See:* the city's sewage engineered away in orderly fashion. *See:* waste and mortality become subject to rational control.)

To address the eighteen-minute exposure time necessary belowground, my brother must first reckon with the living, who cannot hold still. They breathe, they cough and sneeze and live possessing ideas not my brother's own. And so, to enliven his scenes and provide scale, and yet circumvent the living, their breathing and coughing and sneezing, he orders mannequins built.

He costumes and poses them in this netherworld, hefting shovels and operating carts. For the sake of efficiency in the manufacturing of his dummies, my brother's sewer men all look the same. Barrel chested, dark haired. With painted, unseeing eyes, and the bulging brows and heavy jaws befitting those of an extinct, superseded race—a popular notion of our time. Or an enslaved people—by our age's finest minds deemed fit solely for the otherwise-sparkling future's foulest work.

Lifeless, the figures fly to me in dreams.

They ascend on the mists of post-drink fevers, curiously animate in their underworld caverns. I rise too, throat parched and lips cracked, an unfettered bulge, huge among them. Each one looks like me.

Their presence persists even on days when I am well, at once strange and familiar, like a memory from a future already past, a memory I perceive from an even greater distance ahead in time.

In this far-future tense, I recall that I am ensorcelled, become wood. My wooden chest holds a deadwood heart. Abducted, held against my will, I wonder how long the life I have thought I have lived has not been mine.

Afternoons, I wake from fitful sleep, and wonder what charm or ransom might restore me. Increasingly, I detest mirrors: my eyes stare round and wide, as if painted in permanent astonishment at how far I have come, at my brother's bidding, and here find my end.

°

Not my end. A few more, allow me.

Ever on the leading edge of the latest ideas, my brother undertakes to photograph the insane.

(*See:* "Guillame Duchenne de Bologne performing facial electro-stimulus experiments." The patient appears charged with devastation, shocked from himself, from a shell once humanly habitable. *See:* my brother's work in support of Charcot and cohort's scientific studies of the youngest, most attractive, pliant subjects—the drama of their unplain, tormented faces from among the five thousand epileptics and hysterics at the women's asylum of Salpêtrière. *See:* the *arc-de-cercles* shaped by these poor, seizing incurables, contorted so far backward in their hospital beds—heads reared in the classic aura hysterica, the ecstatic back-bending posture created by catalepsies and deliria—that they resemble flightless balloons of flesh.)

°

(*See also:* my brother claims in his voluminous writings that the photographic pose—for the willing and unwilling, famous and god-forsaken, sensate and not—emulates brain disease. The waves of fear experienced by those who pose motionless before the camera, and who later appear motionless in the print, reduce his models to spectres of themselves. *See:* I am not the only one prone to wishful thinking.)

°

My best photographs? Racehorses. I attend to them at the track. They snort and stamp, and yet I too freeze my subjects, stop time. I too have the gift.

Though my gift of foresight also tells me that this ability, and this notion of the trade, will become a commonplace. Not an art.

At the track the horses whinny, lift their tails and shit, and merely provide somewhat of a living. My afterlife, should I have one, will exist in my photos binned at flea markets, for sale cheap.

°

Years pass. I drink and drink, and yet I scrape together enough to purchase a house in the country. A green refuge, in Sénart, not far south of Paris.

A train takes me there. For hours each day, I lie head ducked beneath the shrubs to avoid thoughts like skies rent by clouds.

I forget de Nerval and Hugo and Sand.

I forget the names, none of my choosing, that I have been called by my brother's admirers: buffoon and layabout, provincial mouse, Maman's boy.

At my green refuge in Sénart, I do not give the time of day to troublemaker and dunce.

Nights, I lie abed and recall much earlier times. Lyons, August 8, 1837. My father dead of an organic illness of the brain. My brother, already the toast of Paris, sends his regrets, unable to attend the burial.

°

I think it is Ernestine who buys the house in Sénart to clear my ever-mounting debts. Is she kind or callous? She installs herself and my brother, and their endless rounds of esteemed, name-calling visitors, I forget who. I must forget they make merry in what was once my place of rest.

Twenty miles south. I remember now. I remember I take the train.

In my bed in Saint-Louis hospital in Paris, where Ernestine and my brother install me, I remember to lie still as an empty glass. My ears ring, bells in a storm.

°

In this one, Chantal, our wet nurse, wipes my chin.

Come here, my brother bellows from the garden.

Milk slides down my throat. I am already four, but not yet big. Chantal's blouse blossoms above her naked breasts. Her hands are huge and red and chapped, rough against my cheek. She kisses the top of my head.

Where are you? my brother the demiurge, ten and tall for his age, demands from among the flower beds and shrubs, most likely preparing to torment the neighbour's cat. Come here at once, my brother brays. Now, when I tell you.

I remain where I am. *Je suis enchanté,* Chantal.

The kitchen window opens onto a breeze. I bloat in it like clothes on a line. At last, I lose my head.

Penetrating Wind Over Open Lake

I left Ewan's office and waited for the lift.

Not enough development, more variation. Where were the bloody progressions, the build? He'd banged his fist on the keyboard of the concert grand a few times, hard. Change, Paisley, change. Do you want me to bean you? The middle section could be the ending or the beginning or fuck what.

I'll add more drones, I'd said, a dig, and he shot me the death look.

My main teacher, Shoshanna from Tel Aviv via Berlin, who I adored for her well-meaning if ineffectual attempts to believe in me and my doctoral dissertation piece, was on sabbatical. Ewan, from Scotland via San Diego, was her heavy-hitter replacement, rumoured to have been snagged for a princely sum, and indeed lordly taking over her capacious, light-filled office, her gleaming and irreproachable Steinway. At each weekly lesson, Ewan sprouted fangs over the slow aching harmonic shifts and the papery, whispering microtonal textures in my duo for mezzo-soparano and electronics. He railed against what he termed my hateful absence of fast metric modulations and my intentional, spiteful lack of timbral differentiation. The performancy performance I hoped to coax from my performer? Fuck no, just fuck no. In case I hadn't got the memo regarding my rearguard reverence for the once-bright lights of minimalism's downtown avant-garde: Who cares? said Ewan. Why should I? he snarked. It's your job to try and make me, he'd goad. Chrissake, Paise, we're on the ass end of an old millennium.

Each weekly lesson I tried not to hate him. I tried to convey as graciously and maturely as I could that I did not want him to bean me.

The elevator doors cranked open. I edged in next to a baby grand en route to the concert hall. The student read-throughs, by the rising-star visiting ensemble, were tonight—only the youngster players for us, and no real audience to speak of—but I reasoned I could squeeze in a quick head home for a bite and lie-down before charging back to have my aspirations again crushed.

I tore east out of the quad and past the library and along the fall streets toward the lake. Toward the apartment. I might be stuck four years deep into teachers and a program that were evolving into a poor fit for me, and I might have no clear idea of how to shepherd my dissertation through to some kind of finish line—woo it into focus, keep the faith that I could—but I could at least love how my legs faithfully carried me forth into the fall, and its reliable promise of new beginnings, with the start of each academic year. No matter what indignities befell me, or flaws I apparently, or in fact embodied, I could chin up and appreciate the flushing trees marauded by flocks of invasive monk parakeets—the oaks and elms hosting with vegetal equanimity the birds' evergreen shrieks, vocalizations that never failed to put me productively in mind of newborns fighting for air in infernal neonatal units, of wildcat singers full-throating like exiled souls very bummed about it. I could wonder: is there an opera in any of this? Even semi-staged? Some day? I took solace in believing the fall, not even this one, in this pre-Y2K time of toxic angst, with the clocks ticking over terrifyingly soon, would never fail me.

I took the apartment building's stairwell steps two at a time up five flights and caught my breath at the door to the apartment. No sound from inside.

I pushed open the door—and shut it as quietly as I could. Raymond sat at his own baby grand, his back to me. The piano's lid was closed, and his score lay unfolded on top, swaths of eraser rubbings easily visible on it from across the cramped room. No electronic keyboard in sight, an instrument far less expensive than a piano. No use of MIDI for generating the score, far less time-consuming than handwriting it, and then having to input every expression marking and articulation into a software program and then tweak the final score and parts. Most of the other student composers, myself included, used this newer technology by now—in fact, I did most of my composing at the department's fully outfitted electronic studio—but Ray would have none of it. For him, only what he deemed the genuine articles, regardless of the costs, in energy expended and dollars, and the sacrifices these costs entailed.

Other than his rigid posture, he appeared not to notice my presence. I smelled sweat. Mine, his.

Hey, Ray-Ray, I said softly, unable to resist—for my benefit, or for his, I couldn't say.

My benefit, my mistake: he thrust a hand toward me at an unnatural angle behind him, and craned his neck farther over the score. I'd seen the gesture before. Interrupt at your peril, it said.

He took back his hand and sounded a series of harmonic motives. Near replicas of those in an earlier piece of mine.

This was a recent thing: Ray repurposing my ideas. Each time I realized it, I'd venture a cautiously neutral comment.

Sounds like you've been listening to my old piano pieces, cool. Sounds like the opening micropolyphony from my bassoon quintet, interesting to see where you'll go with it.

Paisley? he'd say, crinkling his delicate nose, a feature I'd once swooned over. You actually think it's weird we'd influence each other?

He'd swipe the fringe of fine sandy brown hair from his brow, shake his head as if mildly incredulous, wave me off. As in: how could you be so boringly, disappointingly dense as to wonder at the price of coupledom? And so fallible, so untrustworthy as to disbelieve in us as a couple?

My offences exponential. And wholly mine, never his.

This time, I said nothing. The gift of my lessons with Ewan: an add-on organ, incubating inside me, a newfangled feeler with which to intuit the pointlessness of attempts to state my case.

Ray kept his back to me, and squared his shoulders at my intrusion, fists clenched to his thighs.

Yes?

That register, that voice: also familiar.

I slunk to the bedroom. I lay on the bed. Ray's bed. As with the piano. He'd bought the bed frame at IKEA, and an old friend of a friend of his sister had sold him her mattress, well used and too short for us—Ray and I both tall, well-matched by height. I'd gone straight from undergrad into the program, but Ray had office temped for several years, post his master's degree, and saved some bucks. When we moved here, together, miraculously both accepted, and awarded the same fellowship, he'd sold his car, and then bought the piano on consignment, and the few furnishings the apartment sported. We were splitting the rent, using our subsistence-level funds, but the place felt more his than ours.

I put my mind on the ceiling and thought about the future: a warm blanket in a cool white space, all I could come up with. I grew hot, my fingers cold. The real covers, purchased on sale at Walmart, scratched. Stray notes, pounded repetitions—hard rubber balls of my ideas, repurposed—sounded intermittently from the living room. I turned onto my stomach and mashed my face to the pillow.

When I woke, Ray stood in the door frame.

We eating tonight?

His tone: wounded. I had wounded him. The deal was I cooked, he cleaned. His question really was: was I letting him down? Again?

°

At the read-through, Raymond's piano quintet came first.

Torture. The violist couldn't count, her intonation sucked, and the cellist, the cellist was all about his hair—I knew what Ray would, and did, whisper to me at break.

My piece came second last. Also a piano quintet, which I'd completed the past spring.

From the first bars, the violist kept up, and the cellist's hair failed to impede the performance. And the pianist—they channelled their beast of an instrument with clairvoyant brilliance, cleaving to the drone of repeated bass notes like the sustained hum of the terrestrial core, a menace, a Plutonian beauty, around which the violins and viola and cello crept their fondly foolish, meticulous filigree of microtones. Then the string players, well versed and joyous in the use of extended techniques, popped the wood of their bows on strings, tapped soundboards with fingertips. The pianist plunged their arms past the opened lid and plucked and scratched a composed selection of dampened strings, and rapped the soundboard with intricate nested tuplets. Increasingly resonant, snail-paced silences, a slow confetti, obtained among the notes. Then came a longer pause—and then the players sang, quietly, with aching tenderness, each musician simultaneously voicing a series of different, and repeated, words. *Apple. Rain. Boil. Copper. Ache. Here. Here.* Or was it *hear*? Each word then stretched slowly and progressively apart, and the low babble modulated into a soft, repeating weave that, one by one, player by player, ended so quietly as to approach the mysteries of the sub-vocal, and dissolve into air.

I called the work *In Your Eye*. Hearing it entire—the riddlingly simple, stupefying textures, which seemed not to know where or how, as a whole, to end, except slow, very slow, although in this reading too slow even for me, so I did have a comment to offer the players, plus bars seventeen through twenty-six of section three extra pianissimo, please—brought tears to my own eyes, and nearly annihilated my pulse.

At my suggestions, the players took the opening section again, perfectly again, then relaunched section three, a delicate murmur now, very nice. Then the closing, which they took incrementally, thrillingly faster.

Ray had offered nothing to the performers after they'd read his piece—no comments positive or negative, no helpful suggestions. Only a withering, passive aggressive thank-you.

°

We students and our faculty advisers spoke frequently—with varying degrees of knowledge, but always with a dose of terror and awe—of the issue of playability. Could a violinist humanly manage these dense sub-harmonic bowings? This virtuosic solo piece for flute: could any flutist in our solar system muster the breath for the quadruple-forte quintuplet attacks? Knowing, and not knowing, the answers to such questions—and the corollary, the knowing and not knowing the excellent musicians we could consult, who might willingly look over our scores in progress, and say, Yes, I can play this, or, No, I cannot—meant the difference between a train wreck and a stellar performance. Or any performances at all: our expertise or lack thereof, our professionalism, spoke to our growing ability to engender trust among players. To eventually snag commissions, garner fellowships, acclaim. Build careers. Build audiences: they came with the territory, the players serving as curators, tastemakers, scrupulously omniscient when it came to knowing what their particular audiences would respond to best.

Ray knew all this—and yet.

We'd fallen into each other's lives over three summer weeks at the prestigious Clusk residency, our union a swift and intense recognition of like to like—and then, with great and improbable luck, orchestrated our entering the same doctoral program together. Four years and change had now passed since we met. Four years plus over which my once lovely and clever Ray now unlovely and unlovably and alonely worked the extreme outer contours of the New Complexity. My dear, difficult Ray, my Ray eerily and self-destructively too clever for his own good, unfailingly expected the players to perform his knotty thickets of notes as written. Believed that any failure to do so represented no failure on his part.

Each read-through, each increasingly infrequent performance of his work, ripped my heart. Ripped his, apparently, given the post-mortem rants that each time, time and again, fell only on my ears—given his increasing withdrawal from our cohort, our friends, his increasingly shitty and ungenerous absences, as much as he could, from performances of their work.

°

The final read-through ended. Warm applause for we student composers rang out, followed by wild applause for the musicians, for the chance they'd bestowed upon us to hear our works accorded such generous attention and consummate skill.

Ray sat stiff and unmoving. As he had the last time we'd attended a performance, and all the other times this past year—of his work, or mine, or that of our friends. Or of any contemporary composer he considered his sworn enemy for achieving greater success than Ray himself, according to his own rubric.

This time, something large stiffened in me.

This time: I felt a jagged shift in my feelings toward Ray as a tempo change. One with no time signature, impossible to conventionally notate. Indescribable, unless I resorted to extra-musical figurative language: the language of this is like this. Or the language of narrative: this thing, this event happens, and then this. Lazy practices I was training myself, with mixed success, to avoid.

I indulged anyway. Sounds like? A disordered rasp of bees tightening, cohering pre-sting. Ice quickening on a great lake. The sorry tale of my disorienting cruelty, rarely far from the surface of my thoughts, in having rarely visited my mother in the nursing home back home, in another country, a country not so hard visit. A story in which something decidedly does not happen, and my mother is dead now, and deaf to my too-late, too-ambivalent, I love you, I love you, I love yous. As I remained deaf to hers—unvoiced throughout our lives together. Nothings I could ever spirit forth from her.

However those last, those nothings, might sound.

°

I had learned the hard way about my capacity for cruelty. I did not want to be cruel to Ray. I was not. I nudged his shoulder with mine. No response. I lay my hand over his and attempted to interlace our fingers. To convey solidarity with his hurt feelings.

He shook me off—the force of it scared and shamed me. Then he ejected from his seat and scrambled past, knocking my knees, refusing me a chance to find my feet and exit the aisle first, or even to shift sideways to let him pass.

I remained in my seat a long moment, facing the stage's eerie squad of now-empty music stands, while my cohort gathered jackets, offered smiles, hugs, congrats. Then I plodded toward the hall's exit, and joined my friend Noor, my study buds Jacob and Ana, and the rest—some, exhilarated, others disappointed.

The usual. But no one as brazenly dismal, as angry, as the now-vanished Ray.

And then most of we students joined the players and faculty in the lobby, where I heaved with both relief and embarrassment at Ray's continued absence. I did my best to ignore Ewan, and Frosty, Ray's teacher—Faustina, in full, but the nickname served we students well. I scarfed department-funded cheese and crackers and tippled box wine, while Ewan and Frosty shamelessly schmoozed the players in hopes of commissions—mostly crowding out we students trying to get a schmooze in edgewise in hopes of collaborations, and generally just trying to feel out how best to kiss professional ass.

Twenty minutes, half an hour? Took awhile for me to spot Ray. He leaned against a far wall, loitering, as if above The Fray, as he'd taken to labelling the rest of us this past year.

I was in The Fray. I was happy. But I suppressed the urge to shoot him a thumbs-up: moments ago, I'd scored a high compliment from the pianist. A request to pass along any solo pieces I might have for them.

I must have spectacularly failed to suppress enough: Ray glared at me, irradiant with rage. Waiting for me. Held prisoner here, by me.

Let him wait—and then the evening did close, and we all bid our goodbyes. Ewan made a spectacle of it, loudly calling me out as we left—Change, Paisley, change! develop or die!—to the uncertain giggles of my cohort.

I shrugged the insult off. What I dreaded: the walk home with Ray.

°

Walk we did. My car had died my senior year of college, and by this point Ray's was long gone. If we'd had a car, we would have driven. Muggings were unnervingly routine on our scantly trafficked streets, especially at night, though so far Ray and I had escaped that fate. Countered it, I'd once thought, with our shiny, untouchable luck. We used to return from evenings studying at the library, or attending one of the department concerts, or the university's excellent series featuring internationally renowned ensembles and soloists, and I'd feel gloriously pumped, striking through the chancy streets with Ray's arm linked through mine, relishing the good fortune of our similar considerable height and broad-shouldered swagger, our matching long strides. Thunder and shaking, I'd imagined us.

We moved gingerly homeward now, shoulders hunched, through the leafy, nocturnal streets. Whiffs of the fireplace, of fall, issued from the finer homes. A raccoon climbed from a garbage can outside a bookstore, tiny claws uplifted, nose twitching. We faced a stretch of burned-out streetlights, and bumped shoulders once, by accident, and quickly shuffled apart, and then doggedly kept on, making no move to turn toward a more secure route.

We weren't working.

°

I'd long known about making things work.

Growing up, I'd been unusually tall for my age, at any age. Big-boned, eventually hippy—as I would remain. Too powerful, I'd seemed to myself in those early years. A great lummox, supersized in my small suburb of inexpensive bungalows and skipping ropes and playing house. I preferred to cruise the sidewalks with a frayed towel tucked into the back collar of my shirt, a homely superhero. Or to crash through the public swimming pool all summer long. Winters I played goalie at the hockey rink with the boys, when they needed one and I was all that was on tap. I ate nearly everything in sight, my mother used to bitterly claim—my hollow-eyed mom, who stretched every paycheque to feed the two of us. The days leading up to each new pay period were the worst: she'd fix sandwiches for dinner, from slices of white bread bought on sale, spread with a thin layer of reduced-to-sell margarine sprinkled with sugar.

I grew anyway, I towered. Never complained. Punched through, as needed, on the playgrounds and schoolyard. At the beginning of seventh grade, my music teacher, Mr Darby, assigned me to the school's precious tam-tam and timpani and marimba, gifted to the music department by an alum made good—Mr Darby snickering into his sleeve at the thought of a girl, even one already as statuesque as myself, making a fool of herself in the attempt. I showed him, though. I showed everyone who'd doubted. Learned to play unfalteringly, with speed and accuracy, and a surprising—Mr Darby couldn't help but exclaim—sensitivity. Played like nobody's business.

°

The walk back to the apartment took forever. My hopefulness greyed, lockstep with Ray's moody silence. A sense of injury—of myself being unfairly taken down a notch—roosted in me. I matched his faltering, aggrieved gait, aware of the screechy, bombastic parakeets, those invasive marauders, snoozing in the tree branches above us.

I'd sometimes felt frantic at the thought of passing injury on to others, to Ray, after my mother died. As if my swollen sadness and anger and frustration could catch. So I imagined myself shrinking bug-small. I'd willingly muted my own words: no back-talk. Let my compositions speak for me, if I needed to speak at all—though I also mostly rejected, tried to reject, such a fuzzy, non-rigorous conception of my work. Outside of my work, a dead-zone bubble encased me, a protective acoustic nullity—the sensation not altogether unpleasant. Confinement meant safety.

But too many pressures competed inside me now. Ewan, Ray. My dissertation piece. Which I needed to complete. And find a performer to perform and record it. And then I needed to beg faculty to join my thesis defence committee, and then I had to defend my piece to them. And I needed a job for the fall, preferably a teaching gig, even though I'd likely be ABD, having yet to defend my thesis.

Panic clawed my throat, just thinking. I needed to get through it all—needed more than I was getting. Was there some miracle drug, better teacher, better boyfriend?

My silence deepened, darkened. It seethed.

°

The calls started again early the next morning. A tumbling, buzzy flock of them roistering on our answering machine. I was accustomed to the disturbance, and stayed in bed, pretending to sleep—keeping out of Ray's way, while he ignored the phone and wiped his ass and drank his juice. Soon he'd cram a wad of notebooks into his backpack, and sigh loud enough for the undergrads in the dorm next door to our building to hear and potentially trill out their windows after him—Poor baby! He needed it, didn't he? The commiseration, the witness: I was too tired and pissed to help him out, even though he'd soon enter the school library and bleed his eyes out on a slamming excess of musicology and theory papers related to the assigned Wagner, Schubert, Ravel, Mozart, Monteverdi, Gluck, Ives. Ray had failed the comprehensive oral exams the previous year and possessed but one more chance to retake them and pass. I'd passed, first go-round, one more injurious circumstance for Ray to contend with—and so I knew better than to poke my buzzy head out of the covers and say, Ray, pick up, for crap's sake, why can't you pick up and speak with your mother?

Ray in the shower. Ray clattering dishes into the dish rack. Our phone and answering machine on our tiny, shared desk, a pandemonium of squawks and shrieks. Of shoes and hats his mother couldn't afford. The poor-baby, brother-sister dachshunds she wanted to adopt, could Ray help her out, fly out to Shoshone and drive her hours northwest, so she could pick the poor babies up?

I stretched my legs cautiously under the sheets, rotated my ankles, flexed my toes. I stared at the window blinds, swallowed a dry cough. Pick up, Ray, I did not call out. Please, I beg you, pick up.

My mother so did not call.

°

The apartment door shut. I swung off Ray's shitty mattress, and stepped onto the floor, into the opulent quiet as if bearing a velvet pouch into a palace. I dug into the far back of my underwear drawer in our shared dresser. At least I had my own drawer for suchlike, and not only the jumble of our combined clothes elsewhere—Ray was finicky about mixing with my private, potentially gamy personal wear.

I sat cross-legged under Ray's piano—the most open space in the living room—and emptied the real pouch of its coins and tossed them.

I stealth-consulted the I Ching every day. What would Ewan say, if he knew? I could imagine his amusement. Oh, the ironies: Paisley metabolizing the ancient *Book of Changes* in her compositions. I could imagine his scorn. He'd accuse me of aping John Cage. Aping his methods from the middle of this near-exhausted century. Way to go, Paisley, Ewan might say, nice work greeting a new millennium. Cage-lite, Ewan might call me, for adopting an approach to using the I Ching as a compositional tool in a far less systematic and complex and spiritual way.

Who the fuck do you think you are, anyway? Ewan might say.

Probably I'd never hear the end, if I came clean to him. Like I ever would.

Hexagram 30: this morning's throw. I consulted the two books I'd also slipped from my drawer and had stacked by my side.

Clarity. Fire Over Fire. Luminosity, or Clinging, depending on the translation. Advantage in correct persistence. Cultivate intelligence. Recognize the times and work quietly and diligently. Avoid useless struggling. Care of the cow brings good fortune.

I'd long known about caring for the cow. If I didn't, who else would?

Not Ewan, with his name-calling—farter-arounder, ding-dong, among the choicest labels he'd bestowed upon me.

Not Shoshanna with her polite and disheartening throat clearings over my scores at each weekly lesson, when she was infrequently in town even on non-sabbatical years. Glamorous and untouchable Shoshanna. Kind, yes, but to a small extent rather than an expanse, and so often missing in action, in Buenos Aires or New Orleans or New York for a premiere this, master class that.

And, and: my poor, troubled Ray.

I was on my own. Or, rather, not. Fire over fire: this morning's hexagram burned clear. Two hot hearts—mine, and my piece's—feeding each other's flame.

More metaphor. Pure impurity. I seemed addicted, couldn't help myself. Wake up, Paisley, I could imagine Ewan saying, if he knew what I was up to—knew the way I worked. Music doesn't *mean*, Paisley. At least, not in this way. What special kind of yokel are you?

Well. I gathered the coins and slipped them into their pouch, and then returned them, along with the two books, to my underwear drawer.

I sat at the desk and unfolded my score. A silver disk of the great lake, visible through our living room window and the branches of the tree beyond—all we could ever see of the nearby water—accompanied me. A near sentience: fanciful of me, I knew. Pure cheese.

°

I left the apartment before Ray returned and struck out for the department's electronic music studio. Pure October: green parakeets arrowed about the blushing treetops. These birds could live twenty to thirty years. They constructed colossal, multifamily stick nests on the electrical power poles, which kept the creatures warm in winter, but also caused fires. Sure enough, two blocks into my walk: a ComEd truck, lights flashing, and a crane bucket cupping a worker, who was removing a massive nest that looked like an incautious game of pick-up sticks. Reminding me that the game, which I'd loved as a kid, had its origins in the I Ching, yarrow stalks once upon an ancient time being used for divinations instead of coins.

The worker worked, and the birds zoomed and squawked pissily around his head. The birds could, in fact, mimic human speech—in captivity. Could capture all our ridiculous, ridiculously human soundings off.

Ewan to me, just last week: trippy dippy.

I'd laughed outright and complimented him on his creativity. And earned a glint of satisfaction from him. A hit of fool's gold. But I took it well—taking what I could get.

Don't get too up on yourself, Ray had phoned to tell me, on a February afternoon four years ago.

I'd left a message for him on his machine that morning. I had the envelope in hand: I too had been accepted to the program. Full ride, including a stipend. Like him.

Don't let it go to your big head, he'd said. Don't think you're so great.

I hung up on him. We lived in different cities then, with a national border between us, couldn't afford to visit each other often, following our Clusk residency. Phoning, talking for hours long distance: our lifeline. But we didn't speak for a week after this call. I'd figure stuff out. Whatever it took. Find a different roomie in that bustling, brawny city to the south, across the border. Open a new bank account, in this foreign currency, and learn, as much as I humanly could, to live with gun culture.

Ray found his way back in with me, two months before our first semester here: mailed me mixtapes of Scandinavian noise-metal bands. I reciprocated with British trip-hop, broken beat. The time came when Ray drove north, crossed the border, and picked me up, all my worldly possessions stuffed into his hatchback.

∘

I swung my arms now and picked up my pace. Leaf blowers blew on lawns, delivery vans delivered, the avian belligerence continued above. I still heard Ray, though: sort of heard him. His post-reading silence. In his silent agony, his dearly wanting to cut me down to size. Cut off my big head. If he only had the nerve.

Could he hear me, as he pored over his Monteverdi and Ives in the library? I wondered if he could hear that I'd increasingly lied to him, wrung myself dry reassuring him about his prospects. Could he hear my feelings for him change?

My growing capacity for deceit surprised but failed to alarm me. I felt instead that I'd gained a fresh superpower. As if I'd found a new tooth in my mouth, and my tongue was exploring the contours, assessing what this tool might be capable of.

Lies, kindnesses. A mixtape of their own. A question of how to weight things. How to interpret.

My mother had taught me how to consult the coins—possibly the most useful thing she'd ever imparted to me. How to interpret them. My mother: before dementia whited her out. Rendered her no longer open to interpretation. Or so open: a blank that I, or anyone, could fill in at will. Make of it, of her, anything I wanted. Anything at all.

°

On my way into the studio I ran into Noor.

How's my girl? she said.

Got a year?

For you, ten! she said, and thrust toward me an admirably hyperkinetic display of jazz hands.

Back at you, I said, not very convincingly, and shamefully stuffed my own hands in my pockets, like a not very good friend.

She pulled a blunt from her jacket pocket and raised her brows. I hesitated, afraid of wasting precious studio time—perennially afraid of how far I might fall—but I was equally afraid of missing out on quality time with someone who actually liked me.

Dearest, I said. Have I told you how much I love you?

Only a thousand times, she said, waving me off. It's too much! Give it a rest, okay?

We found an unoccupied bench along the nearby berm. I drew a tissue from my bag and honked my nose. Smoking—it never didn't get to me. I'd grown up with it: my mother with her cigarettes and weed. A woman turning to smoke, which turned to lung cancer. Which came later in her life, the fog of her late-stage dementia having already set in. When she didn't know what the treatments might be for, what shape she was really in. The shape of her becoming vapour, and eventually ash that the air took when, the summer between Ray and my first and second years in the program, I released her remains somewhere in the Grand Canyon of Pennsylvania, alone on a steep hiking trail, a nice enough place, I'd supposed, while Ray waited by the trailhead in his parked car, which he hadn't yet sold. He'd had a bad cold, hadn't been up to the climb—the whole hour I was gone, he'd kept the motor running, the heat turned on. When I got back to the car, it was almost out of gas, and Ray was beyond pissed. Not at me, he claimed, after much counter-pissed prodding from me. In general pissed.

You okay? Noor asked.

Yeah, it's just. I don't know. Shit.

She slung her arm around my shoulders and rested her head against mine.

I do know.

A few leaves, golden in the light, swayed through the air to lie at our feet. I sighed and groaned, and Noor groaned and sighed, and we laughed. At ourselves. Our world.

Then Noor perked up. You coming tonight? she said.

I'd forgotten. The concert at another school's music department, in a nearby suburb. Interesting programming. Mostly contemporary works, performed by some excellent student players, some of whom I knew. Including one I didn't: a mezzo who'd made finalist at the Gaudeamus competition in Utrecht this past spring. Tonight she'd be singing Berio.

Count on it, I told Noor.

°

The department's electronic studio: a viper's nest of cables and plugs and computers and speakers. A list that did not even begin to do the place justice.

I plugged in my Zip drive and headphones and opened my files. Fire over fire. What I had so far: a coursing but jagged, truncated texture. As of something incomplete. Like a close-up detail from a much larger repeating weave. Also, a layer of machine drones.

And a mezzo part increasingly engaging, fucking with things in dark spirals, a demotic whooping that circled repeatedly back on itself, jarring and jolting agonistically, ecstatically. I conceived of the whole as a brief mono-opera with no words, just sounds. I wanted it performed in a darkened hall, the singer unspotlit and, the idea came to me now, clutching a detuned electric banjo and working its tinny, lo-fi plaint into the mix.

Song—including the expressiveness birds exhibit—preceded spoken language in humans. Made it possible by enlarging the human brain. Enlargement spurred evolution. Of course Ewan was right with his *change, Paisley, change, develop or die.* I was trying to change, develop. By reaching back in phasing loops. And also forward, in the guise of a human voice hurling itself against confinement, creating its own variations. I called my dissertation piece *arc-de-cercle,* and was trying my absolute best, despite Ewan, to realize a non-linear, multidirectional shape and structure.

Absolute music: non-narrative, with the singer voicing a seemingly as-yet invented language. Or a lost language. A secret one.

But my piece did also bear a secret aboutness: a fragment of a story. A true story.

When I was growing up, my mother had this friend. She'd arrive at our house unannounced, driving her rattletrap car onto our cracked drive and nearly onto our lawn, and stay for Diet Cokes and smokes and a tarot reading, another mode my mother was into. Her friend Nan: long, flyaway hair partially obscuring a narrow well-lined face. Soft brown eyes—too soft. A woman pressured, a decade earlier, by a roving, unfaithful husband, and a cadre of psychiatric specialists, to do things their way: electric shock treatments for a debilitating depression. Treatments that turned her inside out, rigid with back-bending pain, left her speech slurred, and thoughts too slow to earn a paycheque post-divorce. Treatments that brooked no cure for the poverty that ensued. Or for the rusty anger and booming sense of infinite loss when, scant years later, another set of docs realized—sorry!—that what she'd suffered from all along was Parkinson's.

Why? my mother asked ten- and eleven- and thirteen-year-old me, forced into keeping her company well past my bedtime on her worst nights, when she parked herself in a chair in the living room outside my bedroom door, and cried herself inside out. Why do some people have it so bad? she'd wail. Why does God even—?

My mother's questions bent over backward, it struck me then as now. How she struggled to make sense of the senseless.

And now, two years after my mother's death: my *arc-de-cercle*. I was trying for a charged suspension, a slo-mo tornado, duration twenty minutes. No resolution, recapitulation. No reconciliation, reckoning. No falling back on the certitudes of centuries of linear form. Instead, broken lines, constant builds and breaks. No one voice, not even the singer's, holding a fixed meaning. Each layer a roving shape-shift. A glimpse of a few threads within a greater whole. No sense of an ending. Not in the sense of a pleasing resting place. Nothing like that in sight.

The mezzo. The machine drones. The electric banjo detuned and fucking the fuck out of things.

°

I waited until the Civic turned north onto the sweeping curves of Lakeshore Drive to make my excuses on Ray's behalf. My usual fallbacks, a cringe habit I hadn't yet broken: he was studying, he had a touch of the stomach flu.

Noor's partner, Birgitte, searched me out in the rearview while she drove. How she did it and remained in her lane was beyond me. Oh, Paisley, she said, galaxies of pity and remonstrance and encouragement in her voice.

Noor twisted around in her front passenger seat as much as her seat belt allowed. He's not your fault, she said.

My gut roiled with embarrassment at my gutless behaviour. Which turned to fear when Noor changed the subject to remind me that the deadline for applying to Take Note, the emerging women composers' residency at Steamboat, was coming up. We'd groused like crazy one night over nachos and a pitcher of margaritas at our neighbourhood's sole and very bad but inexpensive Mexican restaurant about Steamboat's astronomical, beyond-reach costs—Noor and Birgitte, like Ray and me, suffered from a severe case of non-existent family trust funds, unlike a good portion of the classically trained, new-music-world people. Steamboat did offer a colossally competitive dangling carrot of full-ride fellowships—for a mere two composers. Just thinking about it now, in the car, hollowed my head, and for a few seconds only the colossal anti-noise of ash blew through. Then I remembered: Noor and I had talked, that night over drinks and chips, about collaborating on a single-movement hour-long piece we dubbed *Fuck You Up*. Birgitte—with a nearly completed doctorate in statistics under her belt—had ordered another pitcher and put the chances of Noor and me winning the Pulitzer for said work at precisely one hundred and seventeen point seven percent. Or negative that.

In the car now, Noor flapped her hand at me.

Hey you, she said, casting a furious look my way. Paisley! Hello? Get your app together. Don't bail on me now.

Right, I said back to her. No bailing, no bailing. Not now, not ever. And by the way, I should have asked way before, but do you mind if I borrow a banjo?

Noor, raised in rural West Virginia, collected the well-worn and sometimes handmade instruments of the region. Junk to some, priceless vintage to others. She never used them in her own pieces, which instead drew from a recombinant approach to Western musical theatre. Throwbacks to the recordings and old movie adaptions of *Oklahoma!* and *My Fair Lady* that she claimed had romanced her past the forbidding green hollers of white multigenerational lineages, and the sad thin-edged mountain forests left to front the strip mines and deceive the tourists on their fall leaf-peeps. In Noor's view, it was the weird, ironized nostalgias of *Kiss Me, Kate* and *The Music Man* that had fortified her through a cobbled-together high school music ed, and from there into conservatory and now here.

Dah-link, she said, in response to my request, and faced forward in the front passenger seat. She squared her shoulders, taking on a military bearing, while Birgitte expertly negotiated the car past the handsome north lakeshore towers, alien as wealth. Of course you can, Noor said.

°

Fall turned to winter, ice congealed on the lake. I applied for everything, anything. Jobs, fellowships, commissions, awards. I worked daily on my piece. Daily consulted the I Ching—repeatedly throwing a nerve-searing spate of Hexagram 36, Censorship. Fuck. More meek responses to Ray. With steely conviction regarding Ewan merely as a diverting cutup—with any luck, he wouldn't be here next year, wouldn't be on my thesis defence committee.

Censorship. It did made sense for my piece. Instead of forging ahead and finishing, I leaned hard into compressing, trimming, heightening. The confinement and contraction. The wild breaks.

My inadequate cooking kept apace too, and Ray cleaned, and many evenings we hunkered in bed, the TV on and not a word to each other. With lights out, the occasional congress lite. Twinsies, we'd occasionally joked about ourselves when we first got together, though Ray had always seemed to inhabit his body more gracefully than I, Ray balletic in the bedroom to my slapstick. But when sex happened now, it was all claustrophobic scuffle.

I did manage to put a few pounds on my bones, busting my ass on frigid five- or even ten-milers through slush on the lakeshore path, and followed up with a good roam through the neighbourhood's commercial streets, scarfing bargain eats in secret—expenses I could manage to hide from Ray. I'd hit up Ribs 'N' Bibs, Rajun Cajun, Valois with its vast steam-table spreads and huge storefront sign, SEE YOUR FOOD. I saw it all right, all that food. Since coming to this city and moving in with Ray, I'd eaten less than I used to, having also to feed him. Not precisely fair to say, given we were both a hair's breadth from broke—I more so than he—and pooled our stipends for groceries as well as rent, and the cooking was the designated job for which I'd willingly signed on. But his comments sometimes: Did I really need that second helping? Couldn't we save that for lunch tomorrow? As if he kept score of what I took from him. Believed that I did.

When I looked in the bathroom mirror these days, I beheld my gaunt, haggard mother. Especially in the witchy late-night hours, when I was most likely to be struck by ideas, and needing to get them down on paper, and not wanting to wake Ray and provide him with reasons to blame me for the challenges he would claim to face the next day, due to lack of his precious sleep. My mother: finally dead, having died frail, weighing next to nothing, while I selfishly developed and progressed, enlarged myself from the inside, if not out.

Now, as the winter days grew shorter, I ate in secret and grew again. I worked and worked, on my dissertation piece, on my applications. I hustled my fucking ass off.

°

Until, at the end of January, the world as we knew it not having ended with the Y2K rollover, I entertained a morning in which only a small animal woke in my head. Like and unlike my mother, who one morning last year never woke up. Who, unlike Ray's demanding mother, would never call. My mother would never ask to speak with me. Had never asked, not while she was alive. Not about shoes or hats or pets. How or what I was doing.

Instead, this: my mother in the living room chair outside my closed bedroom door when I was a teenager, middle of the night, no longer wailing her pitiable questions. Instead, crooning sorry curses. At her life, me. Waking me in the bed she had bought and never let me forget. How much I had cost her. This diminished, maddening creature driving me into sweats and jacket to sneak past her and out the kitchen door. I'd cut through the neighbourhood, crossing the dark blank of my high school's football field, and let myself into a friend's house—I knew where they kept the spare key—and sit at their kitchen table and finish an essay, study for a test, apply to university, to leave. I did leave, cut out. Only to find, in my scholarship-funded sophomore year, my mother failing to call across the frozen great lake of my hometown, on whose shore I often stood that winter, pregnant and then not, a blank inside me fritzing with hormonal static, me yearning to leave the bad boyfriend, but stalled inside, not knowing how. Knowing only a burgeoning desire, a gaping need, to leave everything—to slide onto the thick ice and tuck myself into the curl of a perfectly frozen wave. A wave with perfect pitch, a lullaby for a forever sleep. My mother—what had she ever been to me? A wave curling over, as if trying to protect only itself.

That long-ago winter passed. I passed. Found a part-time job waiting tables, completed my courses, despite how many classes and lessons I had missed: those days spent riding the bus to the streetcar stop, the streetcar that would ferry me to school—but then crossing the street instead and riding the bus back to the apartment I shared with boyfriend stoner central, and then heading to that cold, white lake. But the job pulled me along, I surfaced, made enough money by summer to ditch the guy and move into a shared house with other music students. I gigged in a local band and then joined a killer percussion ensemble, which led to a well-paying stint as assistant to an opera composer, during which I kicked ass and took names and somehow blasted through my final two years of undergrad.

I remembered: exhilaration, exhaustion. Exhaustion now, this winter, I shut down, stayed in bed the whole day, ignored Ray. The late-January day stretched to a week, into February. I got up to use the bathroom, taste mouthfuls of the garbage soups Ray grudgingly prepared, and glimpse the sliver of this other great lake through the apartment window. The lake grey and semi-frozen in the winter light. An unblinking, gimlet eye. Remember me?

°

So I had my despondency just as Ray had his. One blustery February afternoon we took them for a walk along the icy, treacherous sidewalks. His father was eight years dead, on this very day: this news on our answering machine, courtesy of Ray's mother. Ray and I crossed to the lakeshore path and slipped along it past the ice-bridled waves. Our self-insulating silence contrasted with his mother's second call of the morning: Honey baby, I need a new water heater. Can't you help, please? With Daddy gone and all.

We'd left the apartment just as the machine clicked on for a third message.

We passed another bundled-up human, face contorted with cold. Ray slowed. I fought my impulse to speed up, to try to warm up. I slowed too, but not before Ray reached out a mitt to tap my shoulder, get me to match his step.

I wish she'd stop, he said, barely audible over the freezing wind. Like, disappear.

In this moment as in so many others, Ray's need to say little matched my need to keep moving, and my need to hear. Why share everything with me? When he knew even less than I did about my father. For instance. When Ray seemed to forget I'd lost my own mother, a mother who'd disappeared—vanished into her mind, before she died.

Ray full-stopped. His lashes held frozen tears, as mine did too. What did he want from me now? How about a thought concerning my own father? A thought that wouldn't go far. Unlike Ray, who grew up with a mostly normal dad, I'd never known mine, and I guessed my mother had only barely known him—he was a subject she rarely acknowledged. So I'd mostly known only my mother, or parts of her, to a point to which children should never know a parent.

Ray and I faced off. He snugged deeper into his red parka and I into my blue. It wasn't like it was a game, I thought, checking myself—comparing rough upbringings and parental failings wasn't a competition. That would be some uncool bullshit. The problem lay in the lack of reciprocal interest. The problem was Poor Baby Ray. It was his demanding mom, sure—and it was also his growing insistence that he never got a clean shake, never received the leg-up that those he labelled the panderers got. The branders and simplifiers. He also blamed our Clusk resiency, the pure chance we'd landed there, and then into this stuck-up program, which made bitches of us. My issues with Ewan, and even Shoshanna, why she wasn't doing more to champion me—also proof. We should skip out, forget the whole deal.

The biggest problem, in my view: Ray's *us*, his *we*.

Hello? he said now. Did you not hear me?

Uh-huh, I said.

What? Ray said, raising his voice. I can't hear you. What did you say?

I said interesting, I said.

What chilled me more than the searing, cold day, the bitter wind: that there would ever be anything in my life but these deadening repetitions. Ray's, mine. Struggle, whine, repeat. That I'd become what I feared most: a mind nulled, effaced as my mother's.

I can't fucking hear you, Ray said, his voice sharpening. Speak the fuck up.

I walked on. He caught up, slid on a tricky patch, then caught himself. Great, I thought, stopping again, a few feet away. Just fucking great.

Pull your hood down, he raged, putting out a hand to halt me, chest visibly heaving beneath the padding of his jacket. I can't even tell if you're listening.

Ray, I said. It's windy. It's cold.

I trudged ahead once more, leaving him to his besnotted, squinting face, cheeks cherry red.

Paisley! Do you even care?

I turned. He'd folded his arms across his chest and fisted his mitts in his armpits. He looked like an angry puffball. A cartoon now stalking my way. He drew near and, hovering too close, drew on the scant inches in height he had over me. Ice gummed his nostrils. His breath steamed my face.

Do you even care what I say? he shrieked.

I had exhausted my usuals. My attempts to console, placate. I hardly even cared anymore that he'd been ripping me off, riffing off my ideas. Most likely he would quit, shelve composing altogether, drop the program, bury his darling dreams.

I'm heading back, I said.

The strangled sigh, very on-brand for Ray, one for the cheap seats, swept down my spine.

What arose in response towered, molten. I hereby incinerated the Baby Ray I'd hosted inside me.

I'd refused my mother in the end. I could go on to do anything. Including to someone else. Prime example, Ray.

You coming or not? I said, tossing him an indifferent bone out of the goodness—it sure felt good—of my merciless heart. The one I'd had all along, and now admitted to, and hoped to become better acquainted with, moving forward.

We slipped and slid in tandem once again, an unspoken but rigid cone of outright rejection between us. And when a piece of garbage fluttered across the path, and entered our exclusion zone, I stamped around it, accidentally bumping his hip with mine—I remained a hippy, strong-bodied woman, but clumsy, it was who I was, couldn't be helped. He lurched aside, shoulders high, limbs jutted, like an angular, angry puppet.

No strings attached, I thought.

What the fuck? he bleated, voice strange, high-pitched. You trying to kill me?

White spume frothed in my head.

I lost it then. Sure, Ray, I shouted. I am trying to kill you. You're only now figuring it out?

He jammed his knees together in a crouch, and clapped his hands to his ears, as if to unhear my words.

No one, he bawled. No one has ever been so cruel to me.

I held my ground. He sorted himself out and clambered into the distance. The world spun beneath my frozen feet in a vortex of gorgeous, spinning sounds. Car tires a-swish on the wintry lakeshore drive. Sparrow-chatter in the lakeside trees that the parakeets for some reason never braved. Water I imagined slapping air pockets beneath the lake's frozen surface. A sonic verse greater than Ray and me, our human hurts. Our contempt.

Ray in his red coat shrank, a dot in my vision. A hazily moving target. A not especially interesting thing.

°

The next morning Ray left early.

I threw the coins. Hexagram 21: Biting Through. Aroused consciousness. No possibility of compromise. Eliminate that which creates obstacles. Chaos in current situation. What creates inner discord must be overcome.

I looked over my score. Soon, I told myself. Nearly there.

For one thing, I didn't just know a singer who knew a singer. I now knew a fearless hard-core singer.

I composed the email and pressed send.

°

Ewan's wife—had any of us known he had a wife?—arranged for a Valentine's dinner for the student composers at a restaurant by the lake: a prix fixe early bird special for which we had to be done and out the door by six. Turns out, she was a doc filmmaker on sabbatical, who seemed surprisingly nervous, unsure of herself, disappointingly dim in the light of her much older grandee of a husband. It wasn't hard to feel briefly sorry for, and then ignore her, flatten her into a cautionary figure as we all drank water, instead of stronger stuff, from now-passé plastic Y2K! champagne glasses and endured the hardly festive mood. But dessert was included, which somewhat raised the bar, except the shard of flourless chocolate cake was so dry my throat closed and I choked. When I stopped choking, I hiccupped, tears ran. My body in revolt, revoltingly.

You okay? Ana and Jacob called out from the other end of the long table, and in between dabs of my napkin, I spotted Noor rising from her seat across from me.

I'm okay, I croaked and signaled her to sit. Sorry! I said to everyone.

Ewan shook his head in transparent disgust. Ray, seated next to Frosty and as far from me as possible, assumed the deer-in-headlights position. Frosty at least retained her regal mien. Then waiter brought Ewan the bill, and he spent a long time perusing it, and I was glad for the redirect, the rest of the table observing him in awkward silence.

Finally he pulled out his wallet. I got to my feet before anyone else, scooted behind chairs. Stuff to do. Calls to make. My friends, my whatevers—I felt their grasping breath, the scent of a blood-lust on my neck.

°

Spring sprang sudden and hot. One afternoon in April, Ewan's eyes fell upon my completed score. What is this? he sneered. A breakup piece?

I shrugged. By way of reply, I requested Ewan's permission to conduct my semi-finalist interviews, by phone—miraculously, I did have two lined up—in his-slash-Shoshanna's air-conditioned and professionally appointed office. A leg-up, I explained, that's what I was asking for. A chance to feel professional.

I did not explain that I did not want Ray swinging unannounced through the apartment door and glowering at me from across the room as I twisted my brain in knots trying to brightly answer committee questions.

I was not prepared for Ewan's sick, twisty smile.

No dice, Paisley. You testing me or something?

This clown. I studied the curl of his lip, the shrewd glint in his eye. His non-slip mask of cruelty, of fun at my expense. His impenetrable mask, impossible for me to comprehend the why of. It was simply what it was.

So I did not tell the mask that my situation was not a test. That nothing in my life was or ever had been. I did not tell him to fuck off—recent rumour had it the department was hoping to hire him away from San Diego full time. This coming fall. When with any luck I'd be out the door, gone from here in person—but still ABD. Meaning I might need him to sign off on my dissertation defence.

It was nasty Frosty of all people—though come to think of it, I was white and straight, after all, unlike her most unadvised advisee Noor—who nobly granted me the use of her office, and promised to seal her lips, after I begged her, pretty much on bended knee.

°

I prepped for my interviews. Composed, wrote my final seminar paper. I ran along the lakeshore path. The weather had grown unseasonably parched, but the water, tempting as it looked, remained too cold for the dip I craved.

One evening around dinnertime, Ray had news. His mom had called.

Hardly news, I thought. She called all the time.

Mom, I said, fighting the urge to put a sarcastic question mark to it.

Yes, I said Mom, he said. She has a lead for me.

I dumped a block of sour-smelling tofu into the wok, and added a bag of frozen broccoli, a jar of salsa. Ray had already seated himself on a creaky stool at one end of the L-shaped counter—we didn't have room for a dining table. I crushed and stirred at the stove, kept my back to him. That morning the coins revealed Hexagram 61: Inner Truth. Penetrating Wind Over Open Lake. Inner and outer realms aligning. The wisdom of the part of us that is unchanging and thriving.

Hello? Ray said.

A lead where? I said, voice flat, hating to have my response forced from me.

Near Reno. A start-up music ed program for underserved kids. Poorly funded, but who knows?

This happens when?

This coming fall.

I knew—thought I did. Ray would leave this city, the program, before finishing. Forever drop the doctoral pursuit. Head for the hills, find a supportive wife. They'd sing in a local church choir—better yet, his wife would direct the choir. They'd entertain a kid or two. An unfussy, boring dog.

What he was also saying: he was leaving me.

Frosty's thumbs-up on the idea, he said.

Go Frosty, I replied, trying for uplift. Go Mom.

Thanks for the sarcasm, he said.

I settled our plates on the counter as carefully as I could. He winced anyway.

I'm glad you're still on speaking terms with Mom, I said.

He forked into his food and noisily chewed.

Yeah? he said. At least I have one.

I took care in pulling my seat out. I wondered what I owed him, if I did at all. Probably nothing. I might not need to tell him anything—about my interviews, or if I did end up snagging a position for the coming academic year. If I got in off the waitlist at one of the funded residencies I'd applied for. I parked myself on my seat next to him. Inner and outer aligning. I felt it. The synchrony. The feeling of rightness, everything unfolding as it should. Ray hightailing it from the program, from me, and into the iffy arms of a small, precariously funded desert school. He could feel good about it. A life of service. So could I. His endpoint a place of determination and grit, a good place, worthy of respect—it rinsed clean any sense I had of my own dishonesty. Of feeling guilty about my secretive hustle. My failure to disclose what, fingers crossed, lay ahead, for me. A trajectory that wouldn't include Ray. Maybe we could be friends. Except we wouldn't: who would call who? At best I could think of him fondly? Except it wasn't like he'd even asked about me.

Ray chewed on, ears wriggling, delicate nose pointed downward as he stabbed at his tofu, fork dinging the plate.

You eating or not?

He picked up his water glass and swirled as if it contained wine.

I hopped off my stool, before I could grab the glass from his hand and smash it against the counter. Or worse.

Just tidying up first, I said, and put the wok in the sink. I ran that tap a long time.

What do you think? I asked over my shoulder, once I was done.

When I turned, I could see the disk of lake behind him. Superimposed on it, he appeared pale, ordinarily broad shoulders caved, a question on his face.

Dinner? I said, pointing to the counter between us.

I realized then that I'd never before posed this question to him. I'd never cared.

He considered for a moment, his gaze watery. I felt bad. Who was I to judge his efforts at self-reinvention? One that to me appeared like settling for less, satisfied with second place—as my efforts might to him.

No: no matter my gains, my distinctions, Ray would knock them down. Despite my successes, and I'd had some, a fact to which I clung. And I was close to having more. So close. I felt it. I hoped it. Not that Ray could acknowledge what I'd had. Or, if I told him, what might come.

My sudden urge to gloat nearly knocked me over. So this was the real me, who I had been all along. Hard as Ewan. Ferociously critical, but in service to an attainable goal. A person who'd refused to feel for her mother, refused to love her, and now strove to believe the dead were truly dead. A person who could easily believe the same of the living: Ewan, Shoshanna, Ray, especially Ray, maybe even Noor, dead to me. I could leave them all behind. I was a person who could shut someone down gradually, and not notice until the deed, the terrible damage, the slicing forward and forsaking the old—Change, Paisley!—was done. A paradox, then: this change rode on the wisdom of the unchanging part of me. The part that could go without love. What a superpower.

Ray leaned into the pause, looking askance at his now empty plate. He cleared his throat, he chuckled. Dinner, he said. Between you and me? You don't want to know.

He smirked in an uncanny rip-off of Ewan. Ewan my secret, unknown-to-himself helper. Helping me realize shit. The smirk a dead giveaway of what he and Ray made of me. Where I came from. Where they thought I'd go.

◦

A Tuesday morning in early May. I emailed the mezzo—my mezzo—an attached file of her part. Could she sing it? I also sent the complete score. Did it all make sense? I waited several minutes, and wondered why she hadn't responded. A half hour passed. My scalp crawled with nerves, exultation, desolation, everything—and I laced up and took myself for a ten-miler.

I sweated north along the lakeshore in my shorts and tank top. The horizon stretched out in layers of blue, green, white. A large, low-lipped bowl a person might fill with anything, no permission or favour to ask. Nothing to stop this person. Except for momentarily, in the grand scheme of things, a bad boyfriend or two along the way.

I legged it past the vintage doorman buildings with their once grand pasts, many of these formerly hotels built to accommodate visitors to the world's fair in 1893—Marilyn Monroe and Joe DiMaggio honeymooned in one of them. But I was thinking of my own space, fantasizing a future home. A succession of airy rooms, with unobstructed lakefront views, where I'd compose freely, gloriously solitary, a honeymooner of one, at ease. A hyperborean hideout, with cirrus for neighbours, where I could be apart, above—above even the apartment my mother wished she'd had, instead of having me. The place for which she openly, with great relish, fantasized about abandoning me. Until she abandoned herself to dementia, sad and old and lost among the halls of a public nursing home. Where she took unexpectedly to crooning sweet gibberish at anyone and everyone not so heart-struck they could not, as I could not, bear to listen.

I pushed on. Made time. Toward the dream of a place in the world for who I wanted to be. A someone, a somebody. I picked up my feet and pushed until my thighs burned, my chest clutched, thoughts raced—and it occurred to me that, if my mother had abandoned herself, and I her, and Ray and I betrayed who we'd been together, and if I continued to add link upon faulty link to this anti-chain, might I one day abandon myself? Ditch my pasts, race into a congenital future. If my mother's evident lack of concern for me had been an early symptom of her disease. If my newly revealed expertise at distance would result in the same outcome. Would my life at core form a series of vanishments? My view increasingly attuned to an imaginary high tower, its cirrus-surround become the white horrors of my mother's mind become mine. As if my mind were an inbred response to hers. Caged within a cage, maddeningly replicable, an uncanny nightmare.

And today was supposed to be a good day.

And I literally eye-rolled so hard I grew dizzy.

What would Ewan think, if he knew what was on my mind? Laugh at me. Laugh with me. Try to bean me.

Ewan again. I had to laugh. Had to think—easy breezily, semi-affectionately, with no small degree of tenderness toward my imaginary, and usefully oppositional sounding board—fuck him too.

o

I doubled back, headed south. Galloped and sweated until I couldn't stand the heat of the day, or my own back-bending, backbiting thoughts any longer—and at Promontory Point clambered over the busted-up retaining wall. I perched on one of the giant boulders, stripped off shoes and socks and stuck them like odd leaves, signs of this alien's life, onto jutting branches of rebar.

A drop of a few feet, and the cold shrank my breath. I flipped clumsily onto my back, and flopped my limbs until my blood warmed, and my breathing deepened, my chest opened. I turned onto my belly and stroked straight out, away from the fantasy doorman condos and, farther north, downtown's moneyed bristles of skyscrapers and fuck what.

Out and away. I kicked like nobody's business, until my lungs bellowed soundlessly, thighs and biceps turned to dead weights, a dragging undercurrent—not that the lake had one. Then my body hollowed, lightened, and I rolled with buoyant ease through the chop. If I was thinking about anything, making plans, scheming, it was that I'd swim as far as I could, before—but I didn't know what. No end in sight. No goal. Only a question: whether anyone, a certain someone, a possible somebody, might or might not survive an end. In musical terms, this question, or line of thinking—though thinking's not the right word—would be difficult, if not impossible, to notate. Should I want and try to. To have it make sense, compare to anything else. What I mean: it's not like the lake sang to me or sang, period. It wasn't, it had never been, like that. It wasn't like anything but itself.

Return to Forever

Finally we are old. In the desert, we peruse the orange boxcar. What to make of it? Other than that, we like it very much. We take turns taking selfies against the mirror-slick surface. Two of us, Toni and Bean, wear shirts in vicious pinks and yellows that disappear in the one-sies, two-sies, three-sies. One of us, Miranda, stands out in black, otherwise impractical in the mid-morning heat. Toni and Miranda. Bean and Toni. Our wide bright smiles all together now, despite our disappointment that Jenny Holzer, with whose work we remain enamoured, never showed for this show. Despite what the website and the printed brochures claimed. Something she knew? And we did not and still do not. To discuss later amongst ourselves: had we known, would we have bothered to travel this far by airplane and SUV rental? Made the effort to instead view this installation by a semi-famous artist, and works by the even less known? We wave goodbye to the video crew, who self-importantly shooed us when we wandered beneath their lights and before their cameras, the director and assistant director and gaffer and wardrobe assistant and whoever else, who schooled into urgent scrums when we stole peeks inside their enormous coolers of iced drinks and tiny snacks that smelled of nothing. We wave so long to she-to-whom the confederation of big shots would prefer to gift their pristine focus. The singer. Of whose identity, and cusp-of-fame status, the makeup artist has deigned to solemnly apprise us. How, otherwise, would we oldsters know? In the eyes of this multiple-pierced and tatted peacock of a human, this makeup creature who somehow does not, like us, appear to sweat? How else receive word of the song waif, pop Sibyl from a future not ours. A sallow, pouting girl swallowed by a puffy orange suit the wardrobe assistant keeps fussing with, safety pins in mouth. A suit that will also disappear, how well we do know this, when photographed against the boxcar shiny as if dropped from nowhere, outer space, who knows. Somewhere from a time that lasts nothing: tell that to the singer too young to acknowledge us. So long, we sing out regardless. Until we meet again.

°

We make tracks in our rental toward the next installation listed in the brochure, pit stopping along the way in Indio for a regrettably heavy lunch. One of us, Toni, orders a *cerveza, por favor*. At which Miranda, the only one of us fluent in Spanish, rolls her eyes. An order otherwise ill advised, had the other two of us been asked our opinion. Sure enough, later in the afternoon at the picturesque market in Joshua Tree, near the property where we are staying, Toni overenthusiastically spearheads our purchase in triplicate of a highly touted gadget for shredding garlic. Pretty as far as a dish goes. Attractive as the mustachioed man touting it. But a purchase, a desire, also ill advised, for we discover, in prepping for cocktail hour back at the property where we are staying, that the device turns out unable to shred bupkis. For which we all, Toni included, blame Toni. Until Toni calls the other two of us out.

Bahh, she bleats, bah-bahhing and leaning across the patio table toward us. We are on our third drink. We are on our third day. The sun slides down the mountains fast. Bah-bahh, cowards. We other two could have stopped her. The ice in our cocktails melts and we suck that back too, and the other two of us do solemnly confess: we are, we are, bah-bahh. The three of us chime glasses, spill on our shirts and pants. Night falls, ta dum. We dig our bare toes into the warm, white pea gravel. Sounds we don't recognize well from beyond the rental property's fence line. One sound we recognize as a yip. From the box canyon nearby. We think. The canyon outside the park that we read about in our guidebook. The canyon we have agreed to explore tomorrow. Several yips. We think to yip back, to fuck with the yipper, then think better of it. One of us shivers, and another fetches a sweater and tasteful wraps for the other two of us. One of us returns to the kitchen and filches four olives from a jar. On second thought, slides open the glass door to offer the jar—on third thought, slides the door shut and leans her forehead against the glass. The other two of us, those of us still outside, busy ourselves with deciding to smoke one of the pre-rolled we bought yesterday, and further occupy our time in deciding against lighting the backyard firepit. Deciding, doing, deciding to not do. All of us, inside and out, busy bees. Excited to be here. Together at last. As if nothing can stop us now, as if that is our song. Although at home we are also together, somewhat together, in the way of friends who live scant miles apart and see each other for dinner or lunch or at openings, meet for a movie, the occasional walk in the not-far woods. But here is different. Here we are together in a different way. A way that by now, our third day in, we can see or feel, but not necessarily name.

Not necessary. Why should we? Who can make us? Can I borrow your toothbrush? one of the two of us outside suddenly asks, her smile disarming. I've misplaced mine. Misplaced? The other one of the two of us frowns. The one of us inside the house suddenly busies herself with switching off the kitchen light. Calling it a night, time for bed. Unclear as to reasons, other than feeling forgotten, peeved about it. Then she thinks: if they call to me, I will turn the light back on. The thought cheers. A niggle sets in. What if they neglect to call? Outside, the one of us who has not misplaced their toothbrush thinks: toothbrush? What next? The one of us who has misplaced her toothbrush fears she has asked for too much. Inside and out, our frowns double like shadows, though already it is night, and our cocktail napkins lie spent upon the tabletop and the kitchen is dark. Those eerie people-trees lurk beyond the fence. Do they live out their shadow-scripts too? Our thoughts congeal, gloom. The two of us outside craft a determination: forget about firing up the pre-rolled. A breeze lifts the scent of sagebrush and reminds us only of our back-home kitchens, and not of the one of us still inside. A rustling cold hints at the nearby canyon, with its petroglyphs to explore tomorrow. But that is tomorrow, here in no time. In the here and now, the one of us inside flicks on the kitchen light: surprise, surprise. Inside and out, our funny faces make us laugh, and the glass door slides open, and all together now we gather our spent napkins and cloudy cocktail glasses. Bedtime. Near abouts. We putter about the kitchen setting things in order and agree on a lantern to purchase tomorrow, something elegant and practical, and to hell with the too-bothersome firepit. Decisions: done and done. We know all about decisions. We have each of us made them like beds we must now lie in. Beds, especially in the dark of night, like dragged lakes, beds like sore throats, Miranda thinks with her usual creative confusion, a malady for which we know no remedy but for the time, this time, we share. Or hope to. Fingers crossed. Lights out. Sweet dreams, tomorrow in no time. But are we not already having it? The time of our lives?

°

Turns out, one of us sings in the mornings, an irritating habit. One of us grinds her teeth. One of us, the eldest, remains beautiful, and one of us is secretly sad. One of us has clipped her toenails into the soaking tub, and the rest of us, the two who would never clip their toenails into the soaking tub, can't guess which one of us it is, as we have all three of us learned early in life that life is sometimes best when mum's the word.

°

Every morning one of us, Miranda, the eldest and most beautiful among us, likes to sit gabbing on the navy-blue sectional in the otherwise very white living room, mostly going on about people the other two of us do not much know and about whom we care less. All the while, Miranda is thinking: if she moved the end piece a quarter inch, shifted the whole thing to align better with the fireplace. If she moved the framed psychedelic print with its molten colors from the kitchen, if she leaned the hot print on the fireplace mantel and moved the flokati from the floor to the armchair. Perfect. She closes her eyes. No really, perff. She pauses to drink her coffee, cold now from her gabbing and thinking. The other two of us have consumed our coffee hot, as we are slower to wake and talk and think first thing. Besides, today's real topic, as determined by Miranda, is sex: don't let the door hit you on the way out. Well: the other two of us might not feel moved to chime in, but we do have thoughts, do not get us wrong, each of the three of us possesses, in her storehouse of experiences, all manner—well, many manners, catalogues of congress, we could say but don't. What we mean is, and this we say aloud: we could wear buttons on our lapels. Buttons with slogans, or gnomic shapes. We all three agree: buttons, but only on the lapels of stylish, ironic jackets. How very us. We smirk our best smirks. Laugh our tart laughs meticulously and perfectly chosen from among our quiver of laughs. Us to a T.

°

We put the canyon on hold to shower and dress with carefree care, and drive in our rental to the Vons in Yucca Valley to pick up more supplies. On the way, we discuss the kitty and how to handle it moving forward. Each of us has already chipped in three twenties, but we have already run out and only been here two days. Only two? Can that be right? Three days, three twenties, or was it four apiece? Where did they go? The twenties, the days. Before we resolve the issue, or at least one of them, Miranda announces from the back seat, her preferred position, that she would prefer that the other two of us, Toni and Bean, call her Manda. What does this have to do with the kitty? Manda? Miranda-turned-Manda, who three or only two days ago, when we first arrived and sallied forth to purchase groceries, chonked huge containers of cole slaw awash in gooey mayonnaise and frightful additives into our cart, cole slaw we all three have so far declined to eat. To be real, the other two of us cannot begin to imagine what she, Miranda-now-Manda, was thinking. The other two of us cannot even begin to think what next. Frozen Tater Tots. Pudding cups. Manda? Not a thing the other two of us would ever want to pass our lips.

°

To make up, we lunch at the cute café on the JT main street. We split the bill three ways, then head back to the rental property and change our footwear. Ready? The box canyon, at long last. A tall elegance, an intrigue of shapes. Startled quail. Wait—we've forgotten to purchase our lantern. Our hoped-for practical and elegant lantern. Now we must forget the canyon has but a single exit and that we will too soon again take in the same sights. Bummer. We must also forget, but gladly, that this canyon's high walls apparently, as promised by our guidebook, culminate in a third high wall, and thereby encloses us on three sides. We must set aside the thoughts that, in our drama-imaginings, we have each of us spoken aloud and together hooted at in overperformed merriment during the brief ride over. Now we enact a hushed hesitance. The canyon's egress lies both behind and in front of us now, as we have yet to act, retrace our steps. We have time to decide that this site, like the competent and humane therapists with whom we have long been familiar, can help us express, and contain and neutralize, our fears. Whew. Thanks. A lot. Begone all terrors of flood and fire and falling from a great height. Of punishing regret and bygones. Let us proceed, bypassing our ordinary, mortal scares. Speaking of mortal: we check the time on our phones, before we arrive back at the parked SUV. How are we doing for time? Too late now to drive back to Yucca Valley and search every last store, if need be, for a practical and elegant lantern, and drop it off at the property at which we are staying, and then return to the canyon and approach the mysterious, age-old petroglyphs that lie farther on, ahead of us if we had kept going, behind us now. Behind us this art we have yet to view, just as we have yet to fully apprehend the effect of the rock cliffs that box us in on three sides. Nor have we taken the measure of this time that is more, it seems, like the shadow of time. Swift, cutting. No time at all. Toni shudders. Bean wishes she had brought a wrap. Miranda-Manda thinks nothing at all. Or if she does, she thinks no longer in terms of the fine lines she would draw feelingly in charcoal on paper, a caressing tracery of the canyon's high walls, the seams of rock and scrub growth that nick the surface, the hollows in the rock face like vertical pools, mini-oceans she would cross-hatch in. Her mind instead draws repeated loops and cross-outs. A dark nest of uncertainty. Dark lines falling, or is it rising, toward a greater darkness. Risk beyond fear. Manda? the other two of us call to her now, for she has wandered ahead, behind. Possibly, punishingly, off the path. Manda, come back. Manda, clad in her usual punishing black, so impractical for a hike in a desert canyon, ignores us. She paces toward the third wall, but off trail and away from the exit that lies in front of or behind us, depending. Manda and the Third Wall: it sounds like the title of a song the other two of us might write, if we were inclined. A foolish song of Manda's single-minded convergence march, a brash composition with a sixties punk edge to prove we too were young once. Manda's foolery—it is as if we other two were no longer here. For which, in this moment, we cannot forgive her.

°

To make up, we say to hell with the lantern, and take long showers, and pick up takeout pizzas and prepare tossed salad for dinner. We pour the wine and decide to eat inside tonight. We laugh, even Manda cracks up, about Manda forging ahead this afternoon, off-tracking like nobody's business, not even her own: too easy, we have read in our guidebook, to get lost in this desert, mistake non-paths for paths, die for want of water. Funny, and not. Fortunately our laugh is a good long one that lubricates our throats. We might just burst into—dear gods, anything but song. Especially the terrible tune one of us sings in the mornings. The insufferably famous one that at least one of us can't stand, the one that Toni or Bean trills. Not Manda. We all know, even Manda knows, she cannot carry a tune. Better to burst into flame than hear Manda sing. Or hear anyone warble that number. Better to fire up, as if we three are witches crackling in a fire of our own choosing, and talk of the flame of each of our life's work. We begin, we warm to the subject. An old one for us. We—but wait. Now Manda can't remember why we have come here. She cannot recall the installations in the desert, nor our friendship, nor what this place is called, if it even possesses a name. Worse, which bed is hers to lie in tonight. The other two of us, the younger and less beautiful of us, pat her hand, lead her to her seat at the table, we laugh, not at her, but reassuringly with. We put a slice of margherita on her plate. Another with olives and lemon. Dear Manda: fear not. You are hardly alone. It turns out that Toni, it was Toni who had misplaced her toothbrush, and Toni has forgotten to buy another, and must again borrow Bean's. And when Bean did her daily crossword after her long shower? She forgot the four-letter word for twilight, begins with *d*. So let us laugh it all off. As we have always done, even the one of us who is sometimes secretly sad, for our mouths groove easily into faces not so different from the ones we bore at grad school, where we first met, and made drawings we thought would change the world. And they did, our drawings, our sculptures and videos and textile pieces, they changed us, our worlds. Our work birthed our bright smiles at openings, solo and in groups, and our delight at the work of ours that sold, and the pops of corks from bottles of decent-enough bubbly, and nice-enough cheese and fruit trays and those punishingly addictive lemon squares. And the special smiles reserved for our best students. And our other smiles, for our terrible students, the terrors who, despite ourselves, stole our worst hearts and our best. Through them we learned courage. Learned that our own best and worst are one and the same. The result: our stamina is faith. Our ambition, hope. Easier to bear than sorrow. Than trying to outstare it, Bean thinks, polishing off her third slice, from which she has picked off the olives, and arranged them in a neat pile on her plate for Toni or Manda to pick at. Sure thing, she says to another slug of wine, all the while itching to slide open the glass door and light up that firepit, truth be told. Though she won't: neither tell nor light up the pit. A point of pride, an iron belief in her inner restraint. Otherwise, what? Contagion, an uprush of florid heat seeking, of blaze and combust. A pyre, she thinks, but whose? An inferno of the damned: good gods, the very thought. But why the thought? The reason won't come to her.

°

We clean up after ourselves. We wipe away the last of our laugh-tears with the backs of our hands and rinse the wineglasses and stow them in the dishwasher with the dishes and cutlery, done and done. Toni pours us each a glass of water from the filtered-water thingy. On second thought, she removes the thingy's top, judges the reservoir nearly empty. We need to fill the thingy, she says. Manda, who has of a sudden recovered herself, Manda the older and more beautiful, knows what the thingy is called, she thinks, suddenly smug with a sense of tremendous accomplishment. She fills the two-cup measuring cup at the sink, which we use to fill the thingy, whose name she knows, the shape of its name, but refuses to say, or try to: why should she, who can make her? But does she know? A stagger in her mind. A scoop like a dancer's stumble-step, a stumble covered up as a step. Why is it so dark in here? Like a veil covering her face. Did she forget her manners and turn off the kitchen light again? How long has she, have we, been here? Why here?

°

Bean runs the dishwasher. Forget the firepit, where did she put her own toothbrush? Her toothpaste? She suspects Toni might know, but Bean is afraid to ask. Bean suspects, as she rinses out the salad bowl in the kitchen sink, that the firepit really does need lighting, but Bean is afraid of this too. As much as she fears woods. Not like here. Real woods, in the north. Not so far north as Canada, she's no idiot, but north enough. Pine forest surrounding a trailer. Rags of November leaves wet underfoot. Punishing cold in the air, ache in the nostrils. Until she moves closer in. The heat. The leaping flames like a sorcery of people she has known and might come to know, a sense of the future as the past, and herself a god, though her burn barrel burns stolen firewood and drawings she has made and rejected. Always her own worst critic. Hours pass, scraps of fabric burn in whirling colours, cotton and silk and poly velveteen she has cut out with her own scissors sharp. Her work. Her work. She feeds the burn barrel thingy, its thousand flickering tongues. She tips a bottle to her lips, her throat burns. Has she ever been happier? Night, Bean, Manda says, and gives Bean a good-night hug. A good thing, given the ancient cold, the fire, a touchstone night that seared Bean's pact with her future, with better work to come from the Bean that Bean Gershon has in no time become. A night Bean would like to reach back to and touch. In doing so, discover what next. Night, Bean, Toni says, and moves in for a hair ruffle. Night, the old fire's fearsome spell. Night, all: Manda recovers herself and finds her room, her bed, and Toni finds hers, and Bean hers, but in a panic that smokes her throat she quickly gets up again, and makes her way to the kitchen, and slides open the glass door. On second thought, closes it. The firepit, she thinks. Her burn barrel. Her bed.

°

We lie awake in our separate beds. We will visit the box canyon again, tomorrow. A proper visit, because it lies outside the park proper: we like that about it. Also, its nearness. Its proximate mystery like the beads of sweat that tickled our backs when we viewed the orange boxcar in the desert two or three or four days ago now. The art installation that tickled our fancy as much as our comprehension. The youthful singer who ignored us. And who, clad in her puffy orange suit, would disappear, fused to the orange boxcar when her crew photographed her lip-synching and hip swiveling. How well we knew only her lips and face would show. And tomorrow? If it is like ours—well. Who knows? For our part, we will return refreshed from our visit to the canyon, with its age-old enigmas, and laugh about buttons with slogans or gnomic shapes, and sex itself, which each of us suspects the others still have, nasty or tender or dull or proud or sad. Proud at still reaching for those badge-bright stars. Tomorrow: we laugh off Kegel and the astonishing price of cauliflower, then narrow our eyes and laugh with cooler rue, not so funny the rise of fascism and flood and fire. In our lifetimes. Who would have thought? Well, regarding fascism: Bean, for one. But she declines, with hard-won and heart-sore wisdom, to chip in her three cents. Ten-year-old Bean called a dirty Jew by the neighbour boy whose parents were German. Not that all Germans—and besides, that was a different era. Facts Bean has known for ages. Nor does she share tomorrow her hard-won thoughts concerning Boycott, Divestment, and Sanctions, having refused to ever again experience the eye glaze that overcomes the other two of us when the subject arises. Tomorrow Toni refuses to voice her regret concerning the distractions of colour and her invisible cloak of sadness, with its fine embroidery, sadness at the ascendance of colour when she has committed her life to black and white, to palladium print. Tomorrow Manda steadies herself against the seductions of light on water, the mesmerizing, infinite patterns, their surface and substance into which she could fall forever, and drink and drown in. Manda who fears she is finished as an artist, has forever feared, even when she was just starting out, afraid her best work lay and still lies vanishingly far behind her. A memory glint in her former near-god eye. When what could be farther from the truth? Although the other two of us remain mum on the subject. And the subject of the most recent stellar review of her most recent stellar show. We remain silent with the exception of wry moues shared between the two of us over coffee back home. Envious, much? No: tomorrow we laugh, all together now with our bright binding smiles. We find a binding topic: what's her name. Our other good friend. How could we forget? Tips of our tongues. All together, a snap of our fingers. Poor Ivy, we crow. Not funny, we check ourselves. So sad, we remember. At least we're not like poor Ivy, we agree. Poor Ivy mad with memory loss and shut away on her mostly lonesome in that hideous assisted-living deal. An unspectacular fail we also find hard to forgive.

°

All that, tomorrow. Tonight, we lie in our separate beds and breathe easy. Forget thinking. Forget our return flight number, if we ever knew it, forget what airline we booked with, what airport we fly home from, where home is. Two of us forget whether the other one of us is called Miranda or Manda. Our breathing slows and all three of us forget our own names. Our tomorrow plans. Our pleases and thank-yous for what we have, and which beds we are in, beds like shadows in the canyon, we remember it now, the one that is a box whose seams reach so high it hurts our necks to imagine. Better to run our hands over the seams as if we are that tall, giants with large distant hands that tower above us and move smooth as fish through the water that once carved the canyon. As Manda in her fertile, creative confusions would have it. Manda-once-Miranda whose flippy-floppy concepts and unbounded implementation plans for her installations the other two of us could never quite grasp. Disasters, the other two of us feared. Until surprise, surprise: brava, bella, brava. In the loosely paraphrased words of a noted critic, in a brief, recent review of her recent retrospective, in an influential and national general interest magazine: Miranda Aguilar's body of work at once oblique, spontaneous, instinctive, and yet somehow perfected, a perfected oblique, one for the ages, mystery wrapped in lustrous robes. From our dreaming beds now: yip yip to that.

°

Good morning, sunshine, someone's up early. Coffee's on, jackrabbit outside the sliding glass door. Where? Over there. Okay if I borrow your toothbrush? Manda's turn to frown. Ask Bean? Manda asks. A long shower for each of us, one after the other, each of us stopping our ears to the siren song of the improbably large soaking tub, a steep-sided abomination, a challenge to step in and out of without slipping and breaking a wrist or worse. One of us sings in the shower: a Beatles song, the worst one, according to the one of us who hates the Beatles and must grind her teeth. The idiot song about loving and doing and doing. Enough already, please, she will never be the same again if required to listen to that song one more time. She will mock, show no mercy, never mind yipping she will throw her head back in full-throated howl. And who among us wants that?

°

To recover, more coffee. A pre-lunch. Let the canyon wait. We sack out on the couch. This time, forget Manda, it is Toni who takes the floor. The topic none other than Ivy Segal: we really loved her. Love her, Bean corrects. Or course we do, nothing but undying love for our irascible, judgy friend. Oftentimes silent. Then watch out. Watch. The fuck. Out. Toni herself has never forgotten the surprise lash. It arose concerning the time she met the king of Bhutan, stop her if we've heard this one, Toni hiking on a mountain in that lovely country, and who should show up but the king on a mountain bike, surrounded by his security detail, also mounted on bikes, and Toni in her hiking dress. The king graciously dismounts to greet her. Thanks her, Toni Wakefield, for helping his people, upon learning that, for six weeks of her sabbatical semester, Toni is there on a special visa to teach video filmmaking to the lovely people of his beautiful, sequestered nation. Does Toni not rock? Not to Ivy. A hiking dress? You have got to be kidding. Who did you think you were? The queen? Ivy skewering, merciless, leaving an aftermath of a dress Toni has long since donated to Goodwill. So that is Ivy. Done and done. Toni heaves a sigh and sinks back into the sectional's deep cushions, sips her cold coffee. The other two of us seize our chance to fight politely over which of us most wants to make more coffee, fearing that Toni's tale papers over a tougher one, and will soon elicit Toni's need to revisit and possibly revise. How much stock to place in Toni's tales in the first place is a question that sometimes lingers in our two minds. A question we push now from our two heads—too uncharitable, a question Ivy might have planted in us. Toni does rock, of course she does. But please, enough, okay? Too much conflict for we conflict avoidant. Too late: Toni puts her coffee cup down. Did we know she once entertained plans to write a book? About a famed nineteenth-century photographer's younger and less garlanded brother, a tome that would generate a reconsideration of his place in the pantheon of influencers on the then-nascent art form. And Ivy on the down-low beat Toni to it? Not with a tome, not Ivy's style. But a story, a fiction, for the gods' sakes. Some made-up crap, unfavourable to the younger brother. Beat Toni to a pulp, it did: a tale of woe. The other two of us scramble to our feet: coffee making, who knew it could be so complicated? That two heads would be better than one for such a task? Fearing what next. Too late: the fourth story in Ivy's latest book, and probably the last book Ivy will ever write, thank the gods, our truth be told. Unlucky four. And another of Ivy's stories: the three of us only loosely camouflaged, damningly present and accounted for. Pasts pillaged, rendered as backstory, motivation, drive. But twisted into characters not really us, bits and bobs stitched into monstrous amalgamations and set loose to err and hurt, hoisted onto ungainly hind legs to blunder about before our good friend the insidious assassin pulps us, story over. After all the years we've known her. All we've shared and entrusted her with. Our thoughts and memories, though only in parts and not wholes. But please. Do not get us really started, we are hardly like spiteful Ivy in her lurking spiteful silence, like the true Scorpio she was. Is. Stinging us into print. Our selves shaken, soiled. Recalibrated, shadowed by corrosive doubts, about Ivy, our friendships, who each of us is. Why rehash? Our dear Ivy is nearly dearly departed. Ivy, whose last book several critics noted for its refined savagery and formal iconoclasm. Its iridescent conjuration, according to one critic, who singled out the story based on the three of us. An alchemical embodiment, the critic gushed, of the punishingly endless galleries and rooms, the twisting corridors, of three artist-characters' minds. Say what? We all three make for the kitchen and prepare more coffee. We fill our water glasses from the thingy and hydrate. Forget our occasional late-night internet searches for news of Ivy's book. Forget flattened, crushed. Besides: most of Ivy's reviews? Tepid at best.

°

Where does the time go? Lunch, followed by more attention to hydration needs and subsequent bathroom visits, to sunscreen and long-sleeve cover-ups, and now look: dusk in the box canyon. A veil of fog. T wrenches around and bangs into M. Or is it B? Concussive, concussed versions of ourselves. Ourselves as buttons with slogans or gnomic shapes pinned to flat planes on which cross-hatches mark the strange light, viscid air. A Gambel's quail hightails into the sagebrush. Our heavy exhalations a greater fog. M twists and bumps into T and B, where the petroglyphs in the narrow seam of the third wall fuse with the darkness. There they are. The petroglyphs. Us: Toni and Bean and Manda. We had all three been starting to wonder. Especially since Manda, the oldest and most beautiful of us, is wearing the black cap she bought in town, it matches her black dress. In terms of visibility, not the best sartorial choice at this time of day, with day shutting down for good. The logo in white on the cap features three stars above a twisted, human-like tree, and though Manda gamely wears it, she cannot figure it out. Why the person-tree. The stars above. Why the black cap she cannot remember buying. Above her cap-bearing head, the seams of the box canyon induce a fast dissolve into blackening sky. She runs her hand over the vanishing rock face. Sturdy enough: grit stings her palms and fingertips. Above the steep walls, another star visible, like a bright seed. An X that marks the spot.

°

Night-night. Again? We have lost track. Tonight, our last night here, we think, we toddle off toward our separate beds, only to find we cannot find them. Here: let us lie together in this large one. One-sie, two-sie, three-sie, all together now. Smiles wide, bright as armour in the days of yore. One of us, Bean, wears her best pair of striped PJs. Stripes for the criminal she is, feeding her burn barrel until it flames out of control and scorches acres of woods. She is never found out, forest-fire forensics being what they are back in the day. But she knows, and that is more than enough to account for her self-restraint. One of us, Toni, flies off her mountaintop. Her hiking dress billows, wind-socking her hither and yon. In the great distance below a sound like glass bells ringing from temples, until, at five years old, she glimpses her father's white knuckling the steel bar of their rocking car atop the Ferris wheel, the single bar that keeps Toni and her father from a fatal plummet. But she is so little, at age five. Might she not slip past the bar and, falling, remember her father dies one lovely day in June when she is seventeen, catching his foot on a broken sidewalk and hitting his head, brain bruised and nerve fibres torn and bleeding. And Toni, with a strange, free-floating sense of guilt, inherits an estate large enough to pay for art school. Which leads to what next and now this. A forsaken dress of glass bells ringing. One of us, Miranda-Manda, dissolves like a witch, like a tablespoon of salt in a pot, water on the boil for pasta, salt she sprinkles illiberally over chopped salad or stirs into her grandmother's famous Mole sauce, dissolves like Manda's skin slipping off courtesy of the long hours she soaks in the tranq tank back home, way out off Security Boulevard, near the Korean spa where she likes to get a facial. Dissolves into the tumour in her head she refuses to talk about, and which might account for her fears concerning her best work receding from view, behind her. The neurologists stymied, Manda's husband, Tadeo, three years deceased now, once confided to the other two of us. Benign, the brain doctors think but are not a hundred percent. Tadeo, who the other two of us, the two of us mostly single and mostly happy about it most of our lives, very much liked. Tadeo a tender and caring and mostly too-soon-forgotten man who left provisions in the will for Manda's care: we liked that he once took the two of us aside, at one of our frequent get-togethers, and told us, as we stood beneath the Japanese maple in their backyard, that we as her good friends should know. About his will, Manda's brain. Does Manda know we know? We cannot know. Tucked together in our bed in the desert, we can only do our best to ignore the yips from the canyon and remember to not remind Manda to miss Tadeo, our guilt tinged with an ironic, incongruous hope: that the engines of our own departures be as swift as Tadeo's bout of aggressive melanoma, of which he never breathed a word to any of us. Not even Manda, not until the very end. The end, the end. Gods' sake: all together on our mattress now, we shift, grind teeth, before we remember to relax. Burn, fly, dissolve: friends, let us agree that not all memories should greet us like queens and kings. Who cares? Why should we? Glass bells ring a lovelier song. Wide bright smiles unfurl a canopy for busy bees.

°

On our last night here, we draw a line under nostalgia. In the box canyon water seeps from below and rises. It floats us on our mattress-raft toward the stars like badges. Is it Manda, the oldest and most beautiful of we three, who rows? Whose work once consisted of fabricating pools and watchtowers, her most mysterious and beautiful of installations. We breathe in unison and mumble in our sleep of smoke and pelicans and apples, toothpaste and wine, a shadow-script we are surprised to discover we know by heart. Coyotes yip in the canyon. Yip yip, we respond in our shadow-sleep. Toni peers down at her legs grown giant. A geometric-patterned dress, retro chic and sweat absorbent, fine for a hike, grazes her calves. Bean's head hurts. Too much smoke she has tended in secret too many years. She reaches her giant hands up, and finds Manda's black cap is far too small, it squeezes Bean's temples. Off it comes, into the burn barrel. Manda rows, with her still-straight back and still-terrible strength, and on the banks of the canyon the ancient, eerie people-trees congregate. Manda rows, and the people-trees salute as we pass by.

°

Done and done. In the morning we pack. One of us finds her toothbrush and toothpaste. Manda grinds coffee beans and forgets to boil the water. The real problem with paradise, we realize, having completed our idiot check before piling into our rental and westering toward the terrible traffic, the absurdly crowded airport, the real problemo is that we have misplaced our good friend Ivy. Is that not the problem? Ivy? We gather on the drive, doors to the now-packed SUV open, and realize we forgot to search under each bed. Forgot to snap back the shower curtain, check deep within the soaking tub, stir the cold ash in the firepit and living room fireplace, ashes left behind by other, less conscientious guests. We do, however, recall our flight number and airline. On the plane now, we buckle into our seats and prepare for takeoff, Ivy beyond rescue at our hands. The realization is like the very cloak of night with its hidden daggers improbably gleaming. A cloak and dagger for each of us three, but at least we are in this together. As much as we are in for yoga and swimming, turmeric and blueberries and walnuts, activities and ambrosia of the gods, if the latest wellness studies we read about in the *NYT* can be believed, and what choice do we have but to believe? Which of us will die first? We would check if we could. Under our economy seats, the row in front and behind, the cockpit if that were permitted. We would reverse course in the rental SUV and return to the bed, soaking tub, unlit firepit in the gravelled backyard. The canyon. Do we have to, in fact, die? Above the clouds, we put our heads together in economy and check. We conclude that, if memory serves, we do not. Our very own mothers, for instance, quarrelsome and lovely as they were, do they not still abide? Like Ivy, we agree. Ivy who once wrote our annals, catching our slightest details, as a ragged fingernail might catch in fine lace, as dishrags of clouds sully a bright sky, Ivy with her lantern-words searching us out: what Manda in her lovable, creative confusion thinks. Although we three would prefer that Ivy never actually find us, search as she may. But she won't, will she? Not really, not now. Not ever again. Ivy existing, as with our sometimes-punishing mothers, in some other place now, where the light is runnelled with dark, as in the box canyon of yesterday, and heaven sent, if only we believed.

A place of peace: we would prefer to buy that. Though technically speaking, Ivy is still among us, somewhat among us, the last time we thought to check. Somewhere in the multiverse. Just not with us. And we, not yet with her, thank the gods.

Sounds Like

Another first day. My ten girls and six boys ignore me. Butts in seats, they face every which way but forward, toward the whiteboard. I wear my blue-striped shirt I ironed myself, clean socks and underwear. The laundry I wash and fold including Claire's. Already Claire busy with next month's lesson plans and schedules for *a cappella* practice and chess club. Her kids adore her. How does she do it? My girls and boys hunch over phones, screen drunk, a choir of connections gusting among only them. They guffaw and snort, I worry about their posture. Their unknowable lives, futures bright or dim. I know that, in our shared near future, every day I stand before them they will unknow me more. Strip me of these pants and shoes. Copy, paste. Delete, delete. Until, randomized, turned phantom, I could be anyone. Their grade eight or four teacher, grade one. Ancient history. Our subject for the year, but in their own way they already know it. But it's first day, so I try to break the ice. How was summer vacay, anyone do anything of interest? No one? Come on. Who knows the answer? Anyone?

°

I uncap the green marker. Write this down. Our very own timeline. What will happen and what next. All the due dates. Come on, you'll want to keep all this in your notes. My girls, my boys? May I have your attention, please? My policy is, no phones allowed in class. Are we clear? Understood? Everyone?

○

At dinner Claire shows me the pictures on her phone. Her students' open mouths, their crooked teeth. A flash of dimple or slick scar. I fork the last of my steak and wait. Unlike Claire I do not take pictures of the first time. Show over, I do the dishes, straighten up. Claire does her yoga, more lesson plans. By the time she's done, it's too late to stream a show. In bed, I struggle to sleep. I listen along with Claire to her breathing app. When she turns it off and rolls over, I try to catch the first calm waves of her breath. A once-regular program I struggle to hear.

○

A new day, new month. Things fall into place. Date, event, this, then this. I uncap the green marker, then switch it for the red. I wave the brush and erase. I know my students' names, though they would never know it. Anyone, the answer? Wave, erase. My students text and check the socials and video footage of I don't want to know, as if from atop a colossal anthill, and I try not to think of them this way. As if some central command tells them they're all in this together, they've been through all this before, they know their place. Not like me.

○

Some nights Claire talks in her sleep. This I hear. This digs into my head. I won't repeat what she says.

°

Already, Thanksgiving break. Up pre-dawn, and then two hours in the gelid dark to the airport, where I drop Claire off. Happy holidays, hon. She slams the truck door. Off she goes. Well thanks, hon, and good luck. Minnesota, fertility treatments, already round two. Good luck with my housebound *Dexter* rewatch binge. Day of, the sweet potato casserole I'll bring to Norm and Shanti's. Drink a beer. Sure, I'll take a drumstick. Thanks a bunch, friends.

°

I pick Claire up. The light is twilight blue. How'd things go, honey? How do you think? she snaps. I buzz down my window and the blue air blows in. A few snowflakes. Season's greetings. I wish she'd look at me. I'm sorry, hon, I tell her. Yeah? Well, I'm sorry too.

°

Mornings now, before we step into the cold light of day, Claire holes up in the downstairs bathroom and slides a needle in. She cries, I pack our lunches. She puts her makeup on and I drive us to school. On the ride over we hold mitts. I park in the lot and we trek single-file across the snowpack to the staff entrance, cradling our lunch boxes against our bellies.

°

We've been through this before. The painful injections, her moods. Me on the phone week after week with the insurance company. Me banging the phone against the wall. If we have to pay, then where's the baby, you fucks. Me scaring Claire. Me holding off on foregone conclusions, things falling into place like blanks, oh look, honey, our very own dissolving snowflake. Holding off, holding on. For her sake. The past three years rough on her, she hardly needs me piling on. Not when the problem is her estrogen or tubes, or whatever problem I don't have. But I don't mind, hon, I tell her, I couldn't care less. At which she cries more, late at night from her far side of the bed, curled into herself beneath the covers. For god's sake, hon, I do not say. I do not say, Look at all the money we're forking over. She cries herself to sleep and then talks her sleep talk. Words that lean into me, but with no warmth to them. Her feet paddle the sheets all on their lonesome, all night long.

°

No ladies for lunch today? Nope, planning committee today, the usual girl stuff. Not again. Yep, again. So anyway, cold enough for you? Never mind that, I'm hearing big snow tonight. No snow day, I bet. Christ, remember snow days? Boy, do I ever. Yep. And remind me, how many weeks left? Too many. Plans for break? *Cancun* for break. No shit? Now Big Norm leans back in his chair in the teachers' lounge, balls up his lunch bag and whiffs it toward the garbage can. Nice one. Now I try. Rim shot. Sorry, dude.

°

Late afternoon, always the worst. Things fall into place, all the sleepy-time fuckers with their heavy-lidded eyes glued to their fucking phones. *Cancun*. I uncap the black marker. I try to relate. Snow enough for you? Come on. Anyone?

°

I cook casseroles, stews, I roast all the root veg. Last weeks before winter break. My suffering, sleeping Claire breathes her rooty breath at me from her side of the bed. I lie awake and recall a book I once read. German writer, considered controversial these days. But back then, not so much. Not for things like the protagonist waking in the middle of the night beside his sleeping partner, another Claire, which is why I'm thinking of it. Claire. He penetrates the sleeping Claire, the book puts it. Pure cringe. I think of all the mornings Claire drives a needle in and cries. I'm glad I don't have to do it.

°

Only a week to go until break but hold up. Family emergency. The momster. Apparently sort of. I get the call Wednesday after school while I'm driving home. Thursday I again clock in, wave, erase, because who knows? I've been through this before. I take the Friday off, only the Friday. Go through the solo two-hour schlep to the airport. Inside the airport, people with their knit hats and cozy sleepwear and slippers and me in my parka and snow boots. When my flight lands, there's the rental pickup and another hours-long drive, into the dark green of the pines. A flock of snow geese above the road, and then curls of smoke from the chimney of the cabin deep in the woods, the cabin not yet visible. Pretty as a picture, the smoke, the cabin when it will appear, except I know better. I leave the rental on the plowed road and trek closer through the deep snow. Stamp my boots on the front step. The door swings open. Hope you brought your appetite, hon.

°

I move my spoon around the bowl. She stumps around the kitchen. She smokes. Stubs her smoke out in her own bowl, stew scraped from the sides, and lights another. She's killing me. You're killing me, you know? Nice to see you too, it's not like you ever answer your phone, how else can I get your attention, how long do you think you can stay? Stay?

°

Cancun. I say it aloud while my plane taxis for takeoff. Why not? Fun drinks to sip through straws and make fun of, Claire's mouth rounding, my mouth rounding, our bare and very white shoulders relaxing and pinking beside a nice-enough pool beside a nice-enough beach. How's about it, hon bun? Think we can swing it?

°

Late afternoon when I return, already dark, the house dark. I text Claire a fancy heart, pink with gold stars, even though she's at practice, jabbing the air with her conductor's baton. Not like she even needs it. Not like her kids won't follow her anywhere. Up and down scales and into silly warm-up rounds of row, row, row your boat, rounding their ardent mouths on cue. And on into various chorales, Claire's girls floating their high Gs over the buppety-bup-bup of the newly shaving, newly dropped baritones. Claire drawing everyone out, bringing them forth. Amazing them with the gifts inside them. If only my kids looked at me like that. Claire's slender baton piercing the air. Not the baton I gave her last year for Christmas, either. The gift an antique, ebony with a silver engraved handle, handmade, very fine. I purchased it online from a dealer in Sacramento. Expensive. Maybe illegal, if it were new these days. Claire puncturing the air on Christmas morn with her honey, you shouldn't have. I don't think she's ever used it. Saving it for some special occasion. Sticking with the resin job she ordered cheap from Amazon. Sticking it to me. She must know it hurts, she must know I hate that it hurts me. And all these fancy hearts in pink and purple I text her, some in triplicate and some with googly eyes and lightning bolts? Does she not know what they're for?

∘

Two hours later, Claire texts me back a plain heart. I'm wiping down the kitchen counters, putting away the Instant Pot, I've got her dinner saved in the fridge.

∘

Once I lived in a big city. Hated it. I lived with a girl in those days. A girl of superior gifts, drawn into the net of my hating. I took things too personally, the treachery of her careering, the bluster and blaze, and not just hers, it was the program we were in, everyone on hyper-drive. On the oversurpass, the succeed at all cost. And me on the unsurpass. I hated that I hated. I packed it in. Destination this rural western job, and straightaway met Claire, a straight shot from hate to love. Simple things falling into place, a different program, a place in it for me.

∘

The loneliness here presents a sturdier cold. Endurable, a thing you can count on. Snow here sometimes until damn near June.

°

How many days left?

°

Not many. The hours that I count fall into place. This afternoon, outside the classroom window, gouts of the white stuff. Now that's a squall. Will you look at that? Anyone? I uncap the green marker, the red. Ancient history, anyone? Season's greetings, everyone? Squeak if you can hear me. A wave of the antennae at the ancient alien among you. Hello?

°

I notice her as if I haven't already, except now I notice her in a way I haven't before. A big girl getting even bigger these last months, days, hours. I know her name but she doesn't know that. Ratty, baggy sweater on. Thick mope on what I can make out of the downcast, screen-lit mug. Pregnant? Unknowable. Happy holidays, you all excited or what? Big phone in her big fist. Like fuck, she says to her screen. As in, out loud. As if in answer to my dumb questions-not-really-questions. She says, Like FUUUCK.

°

Things fall into place. An instant, hair's breadth, does that sound about right? In no time I'm abreast her desk and slap her phone to the floor. Did I catch her hand? I caught her hand. With my hand, this arm, which I dead-drop to my side like a lead pipe. Like something I'd use to knock the shit out of something. Weapon I'd bury if I could. Who me? Nothing to see here, folks.

A second for my girl to register what's happened. Like, what the? Then several looks fleet across her face. Which looms, giant, a giant blazing billboard of loom. Of shock. Of maybe she'll let rip and squall like a big hurt baby in wounded fear then anger. Then something else. Anyone? I know, I've got it, the look? Pure glee. Pure I've got you now, sucker. Haha thanks a bunch for the early prezzie. Better than cheap socks.

°

I have tried to live as Claire does. To live in the light of Claire's love for her kids. I have hoped, as she does, to do good by them. To not swear at them out loud, not observe them twitch their antennae at their screens, not slap their fucking phones from their fucking hands. I have endeavoured to appear in my place before them, if not sturdy, durable, endurable, if not there for them, then at least frictionless. An untenanted, benign spectre. And it is in this spirit, hastily re-summoned, at least there is that, that I return now to my desk. My place, at least for now, at the front of class. This place for which I once set aside my old hopes and dreams, and with Claire's help lit new ones. And from where I now must hope to face the challenges to come, in light of what happened and what happens next. How history happens, its forward march. Right? Anyone? The challenge, for example, of my not playing the victim card. Not these days. Remember the old days? Who does anymore? Anyone? Not the principal nor the super. Not pale-faced, suffering Claire.

°

I wonder if my stand-up heart, the one I believed I possessed these past years, will fall down.

°

My girls and boys, you face me now.

°

I scrape my chair from the desk and sit. It's nowhere near lunch-time, but I pour the coffee from my Thermos. I cross my legs and glance at the big clock over the door. Chin up. Class cancelled. Excused. Everyone? Chin up, but the words scrabble and slink out of me. Every big girl and boy twitches their mouth, rounds them, stunned. Then they relax into grins big as years. The kids snort and laugh, click and buzz in their own language. Rear huge from their seats and march past. On their giant hind legs they go.

Take Ten

I, Ivy.

That's right, you're Ivy. Do you remember who I am?

Okay, okay.

Ivy! Honey. Who am I?

Sweetheart.

That's right, Ivy. And you're mine.

Okay.

Try some more pudding cup, Ivy. Tater Tot? Here, just one?

Okay, go.

No, not even one? But okay, you're right, Ivy. I do have to go now. See you tomorrow. To-mor-row. Love you.

°

Hello, my love. How're we doing today? Did you have a good lunch? Did you eat?

GO.

Shh, it's okay, it's okay. Do you want to watch the movie? With the others? Here, I'll wheel you. Here we are, this a good spot? Can you see the screen okay? Hello, Mr Henry. Ivy, can you say hi to Mr Henry?

Okay, okay.

Ivy, come on. Okay, tell you what.

Surprise.

Yes? Here, take my hand. A surprise. To what do I owe?

Ten.

Ten, ten. Let me think. Can you help me out, give me a hint? No? All righty, then. I have a surprise too. Next week's our anniversary. Our anni-ver-sary.

Go. GO. Ten.

Not our tenth. Try ten times *four*. Do you know what ten times four is?

∘

Four dogs at rest, silky and smart. Coursers of rabbits and voles. The dogs' hot tongues hang. Dogs out of reach, not for hand patters, not for a girl of four caged in nice, a girl who'd like to bite the bars, the seeds are already there. The dogs know, best to avoid this one. Above the dogs, four crows on a branch ruffle their plumage. Do they know too? Four the zither of horsefly, ravel of goldenrod, the cracked pot of a girl crotch, hot piss on girl legs. Here comes Mother. Once in a field in June. In the early annals of I, Ivy Segal.

∘

Are you cold? Here, your blanket's slipped. Better?

Okay.

I was thinking. Remember when we went—

Go, go.

Okay, Ivy, do you remember this song? Sing it with me.

GO.

I'm sorry, Ivy. You can't go, this is where you stay now. Look how nice it is, isn't it nice here? Look, there's Mrs Ali. Can you wave at Mrs Ali, Ivy? Yes, hello, Mrs Ali, remember me? Mr Adisa Obasi.

TEN. TEN.

Shit.

°

Ten deities. I, Ivy Segal, made them up. And then, in daring trespass, did sail. And climbed the stone steps, and opened my ten books, and spoke. Some listened, once upon, and some of them dead. Even then. Even so, they asked me to sign their names, below mine. I signed theirs smaller.

°

Sailing. You went sailing, Mom? What's she saying, Dad?

Every evening, she gets worse, Brooke. Sundowning. Too bad you arrived so late and had to see this.

Dad. My flight was *delayed*. But what does she mean, sailing?

Brooke, this is hard, but your mother has a new vocabulary now. This whole past year now, before I even brought her here. You might have known, had you—

Dad, please.

I, Ivy.

That's right, you're Ivy. And this lovely creature beside me is Brooke, your daughter. Can you say hi to Brooke?

Kate. Kate.

She thinks I'm Aunt Kate! No, Mom. It's me, Brooke. Oh, shit, shit.

Here, it's clean. Go on, take it. Do you need to go to the restroom? Just past the nurse's station.

I'm fine, forget it.

GO.

Ivy, sweetheart. I'm sorry. Kate's not here.

I mean, wow, geez. Didn't Kate die when Mom was twelve?

Ten. And try talking to her, Brooke, and not me. And don't whisper.

Good, Mom, sailing.

Your mother never got over it. Never stopped talking about her.

I didn't know.

No, you didn't know. But she talked about Kate with me. Many times.

Oh, okay, Dad.

Look, Brooke, I'm glad you could make it. I know how busy you are. I know this is hard. I know your mother was hard. Those things she wrote. You were young, she thought you wouldn't—

Dad.

And I—

Dad.

It's all love, Brooke. That's all it ever was.

Okay, Saint Dad. If that's what you want to believe.

Saint. Can I quote you on that?

Quote me, yeah, go ahead. Take what I have to say into account. First time for everything.

Brooke.

Dad.

GO.

°

And so I sailed and climbed, I spoke. But a moist sigher paid a portion of my fare. Meaning I had to bring him with. And this other one too. She paid. And paid. Evidently. Given the too much makeup, black sails down her too-bright cheeks. Unlike pale Kate, who *once upon a* brandished a peony. She'd plucked it from a clear glass vase, petals whose colour I, Ivy, could eat. Kate next to Rollie at the head table, and a clear vase at each of the other nine tables at the reception. Ten tables total. Each with their giant fleshy things. Kate brandishing and sniffling and drunk for all to see in a pale blue dress. And Mother mad, of course, always angry, this time at Kate's dress blue as a moon. Blue? I, Ivy, will call Kate and ask. Kate, please confirm. And I, Ivy, shall resolve forever after to not make up, not sort and twist and turn on the stone stairs as I speak. As I, in the annals of I, Ivy Segal, am prone to trespass in this regard.

°

Hello, Ivy! As of today? You are my dear wife of forty-one years! Look, I brought cake. Let's have some cake, won't that be nice? Before lunch, but I won't tell if you don't. Here, let me open the box for you. There. Red velvet, your favourite. Our favourite. We had it at our wedding, remember?

°

Cake? Cake? For Kate's wedding that I, Ivy, made up? Confirmed. No blue dress. No Rollie or peonies. No Kate. Confirmed, a horror best untold in accordance with Mother's ever-after lines drawn, best to not cross. Do not cross the street. Do not speak to a man who rolls alongside and rolls down his window. Ivy, do you hear? Do not cry over spilt milk. Over Kate gone, do you understand? Go, Ivy, you go on, live your life away. Forget spoiled Kate who spilt and carried on over every little thing until she got her way, Kate who could charm the pants off, and never thought to say no to anything. And got her just desserts. And I, Ivy. I—oh, shit, here comes Mother now. A pink-edged hill, a place to not go, her hulk in the hallway. Tiptoe past. Or sail with, when I, Ivy, child of ten and newly sister-less, newly less my sweet sixteen sister, was towed by Mother through the old subway cars and shops to a train to a field dotted with grazing horses. Tails swishing, flanks twitching, large eyes gold. Through the June fields to a forest where possums play alive, ply devil's grins and root at dead tree trunks. To a small meadow beyond the forest. A green secret grave. Four made-up silky dogs and four made-up crows. And I, Ivy, ten years old in the annals of Ivy. I, Ivy, in my green dress, swiping at the hot piss on my legs. See what happens? Mother says. Do you see now?

°

Green? Ten? I'm not getting it, what you're telling me. Look, red velvet. Just a bite? No? Here, should we give some cake to Mrs Ali and Mr Henry? The nurses? Nurse Reyes, hello, Nurse Pritchard, can I leave it for you two and the other nurses? Great, thanks much. Okay, then, that's that. I'll see you tomorrow, Ivy. Okay? Come on now, you're okay. You stay here and I'll go. But I'll see you again, tomorrow, love. And you'll see me too. Doesn't that sound nice? And look, love. Nearly time for lunch.

Witch Well

On a midsummer morning I enter the frozens. Alan: inescapable. He waves energetically from his end by the ice creams, then launches his cart, hands cupped around his mouth. Incoming, he calls out. Clear the decks.

A wobble of wheels across the waxed floor, a faint metal tink where his carriage's nose boops mine. Boop, my friend Alan says.

Not today, Alan, I say. Not today.

As if in a horror flick, he is suddenly right beside me. How did that happen?

Cue the spooky laughter, his. He touches my wrist, as if to summon me. I hold out, unmoved, selecting against the category of good-times gal. His face blanks, then falls, and I roll by.

Dar-la! he screams, trying a new tack, sounding very black and white and Brando and startling the young couple by the tofu scrambles. Hey, Dar-la!

I lift my finger in a backward-facing salute.

Darla Darl, he yodels, and I am not sure whose part he is acting now. Oh, my Darl.

I click my heels along the aisle, hesitate by the microwave stir-fries. I put my nose to the glass. My breath puffs a ghost over my reflection.

Be a doll, Darl, he wheedles. Can't you? Just for once? Let me be here for you.

All it takes is once. If I allow my friend Alan to be here for me, then I must return the favour and be here for my friend Alan: a universal law in these fair parts. Just once is the tipping point. The point of no return.

Last chance, Alan says with a chuckle, his good nature on power display. Offer expires soon, he says.

How soon, I am unsure. I have spaced again, one of the spells I keep experiencing lately. I come to at the waffles, the breakfast burritos. I allow they look pretty good. I admit they remind me of something. A noisy kitchen. Burnt toast. The flutter of small hands waving away curls of smoke. Laughter, cries of *not again*.

Darla?

Having none of it, I gather steam, torque the corner. Poof.

°

I smashed my mailbox. I littered the sidewalks with used facial tissues from here to the outer limits of our mountain stronghold. I begged the neighbour girl who cuts my lawn to miss a few months. At noon I open my front door when the doorbell rings. My friend Kira. She likes to check in after tennis in her sleeveless ensemble, golden hair swept into a high ponytail, the shine of health and happy on her smooth brow.

Special delivery, she says with a smile. Woe is you.

Her Knock 'Em Red nails glisten against the envelope clamped between her thumb and first finger by a corner and outthrust as if it wafts cooties. My mailbox might be malformed, but it still opens, woe is me. A spotted lanternfly, one of the newer invasives, lands on Kira's toned shoulder. Boop, I think, but Kira does not flinch. She never does. Her face is its usual unperturbed porcelain.

Darla Doll? my friend Kira singsongs.

Did I notice her lips move? I did not. A second lanternfly fritters the knife pleats of her short skirt, then alights on her white tennies. The spotted scarlet wings, the black lacquer antennae and legs—my friend Kira does know how to accessorize.

I accept the missive grudgingly, noting the gold-embossed stamp, a conifer ringed by tall peaks, on the envelope's upper front left. I rip the flap and yank out my third Community Standards Checklist, with its vertiginous tower of red checks against me. Code Red.

Kira lifts a pest-clad foot toward my threshold. Oh, honey, she says.

My oppositional reflex kicks in. I cross my arms over my chest. Does my friend Kira not know my troubles are not hers?

She half steps back and shakes out her ponytail, her scent of sunshine and cedar coming at me hard. Of course she knows, but can she not come in? Do I not know that together we can get through this?

I wage my best smile, wan at best. Can my good friend Kira not have a nice day without me?

Her smile could win wars. A smile this implacable and self-possessed and glowy could end global poverty. Kaput child labour. If it felt like it. Or have my back at the next Community Association Meeting, where my other good friends and neighbours might raise a motion to kick my tush off this blessed mountain enclave.

I bang my door shut in Kira's perfectly symmetrical face. Rude of me, but a lower-stakes substitute for slamming my head against the two-inch slab, a feat I have twice recently accomplished with aplomb, only to twice lie in a state in a giant cylinder in our gleaming Community Clinic while massive magnets magnetized my brain. Two times have I dullishly awaited the official verdict: the damage slight, not yet done.

I study the oak grain in front of my nose and reflect on how far I have come in my personal journey.

Call if you need help sorting out the shitshow, is what I think my friend Kira chirps against the shut portal, and I muffle back that I won't.

Darla Darl, everyone needs help at some point, I hear something like Kira's voice fade down my path. At some point, at some point, at some—

No point. No help. Since my arrival in this blessed place, in a time I cannot quite recall, I have done my best to enlighten my friends Kira and Alan and others of their ilk. One afternoon I blared the truth from my slate roof with its handfuls of missing tiles. One moonstruck midnight I preached from the disrepair of my bluestone back patio. Last month—I think it was last month—I crafted, from the disarray of my under-appointed craft room, a misshapen clay figure representing my hopes for succor. Sheer genius. Especially those needles lancing where heart and gut might dwell. For the hell of it I displayed the wizened creature at our monthly Community Art Fair. For hours I stood at attention next to my creation and dared our fine community's folks to look away. Look, I said evilly, on repeat, until not a soul dared come within twenty feet of me. No magic, I proclaimed. Not in this baby.

I space again for a sec. I think? I come to, nosing my front door. I finger the residual bumps on my tenderized skull. Locate a new tender spot. Did I just blow my own mind? Again? Where was I?

Then I spy it. Another lanternfly. It sits tight, alive or dead on the marble floor. Rode in on Kira, I suppose, and slipped past me. Part fly, part moth, to be real about it, if I can trust what I have read or seen on the news. If anyone can trust anything they read or watch on the news. *Lycorma delicatula*. Pure pestilence, according to the drama-llama bulletins. Every inhabitant of our clement town within our iffy state within this whole peevish nation is under a strict injunction to personally aid in extincting these bringers of blight.

I crouch over. Dead or alive? Or just spacing, like me at times.

A shiver of polka-dot wings, like those on an antique, mechanized whimsy: alive, then. Then it refolds its wings and settles, as if for some duration I cannot comprehend.

What I do get: the prettiness. Like the seductions of shiny leather straps on the shiny shoes filling my closets. The gleaming trays of top-flight tuna belly and yellowtail whisked same-day direct to our top chefs who prep the monthly Community Swing-Dings. I might be moved to pee on my closest neighbour's prize rose bushes during each waxing gibbous, or to streak mascara on my next-closest neighbour's lemon-yellow front-porch cushions, in either case sprinkling my personal brand of witch on the mighty nice here—to get more real, to make the case that pretty is not always what pretty does, to speak truth to *something*—but I do occasionally suffer from a bad case of both-sidesism. Of beguiled by beguilements.

I straighten and collect myself. I give the Community Checklist a good flick, as much as I can with my bitten fingernails. The clarity of checklists, the inane ticking off boxes of things to be fixed, stages to move through: it is not as if they ever did me any good or ever will.

The moth-fly remains. I nudge the motionless bauble with my big toe. Well, hello, my pretty.

Sound of silence. Sound of I am on my own.

I lift my foot. It appears huge. Disproportionate to the object of its death-smiting righteousness. I drop my weapon to the floor, wrench my ankle. And gasp, shocked at how good it feels to feel so bad—but by the time I think this thought, the pain is already passing. As pain does in this dazzle town.

The lanternfly, moth-fly, cutie patootie, refuses to bestir. Alive or dead, I let the creature be.

◦

Need help? Marley Uwanawich at your service, give me a ring and your future I will tell, your riches realize, your crap help cut. The big bad sis in Corrections? Owes you and a zil others big time? Do not ask how I know, or how I can fix things. Just kidding, ask me anything! Your wish, my command. Call toll free at 1-800-996-6661. Uwanawich? Count on me.

I reattach the creased flyer using the fridge door magnet. The message remains a muddle. A shaky promise I found push-pinned to some sleepy town's grocery store bulletin board on my long blurry trip to my new home here.

For one thing, my sis Marl (not her real name) is the one doing time. Who did she not bilk? The feds closed her down for larceny, fraud.

For certain other letdowns too, if I had been granted my say at the sentencing. Disappointments a person might not care to name.

Is it true? I wonder. Once a witch always a witch?

But when the appointed time arrives, as I do every day, I place the call. But not to the toll free.

°

Dusk. I clip my fanny pack around my waist, hop into my sporty tank, and wheel it onto the street. The neighbours' accent lights blink on, and their illuminated hollyhock and weeping Japanese maples wave as I go by. Block upon block: pampered riches of expertly pruned dogwood and redbud, streaks of mountain laurel. Everything in bloom, always in bloom. I wave to Izak or Ivor or Ignacio in the security hut by our community's impressive front gate, and hit the main road, cut a quick left onto the service road, left again, sharper left. Ease up at a scramble of hemlock and quaking aspen. Cut the engine, shoulder open the door and slide into the purpling air.

Overhead, swallows stalk mosquitoes, catbirds mew. I set forth and so on, picking a path through a tangle of fallen branches and crushed tallboys, skirt mossy overgrowth on suspicious-seeming mounds. I huff fumes that sting my eyes. Clumps of giant weedy poppies scratch my knees bloody and rag the hem of my darling dress—which is fine, I have closets of these too. I grow bendy limbed, rubbery tall, and soon reach the glade with its low-lipped and crumbling stone enclosure, where I misplace my head. While another part of me, I am not clear which, beholds the brambled and thorn-veiled mouth. My heart too has drifted out of reach, I am untender, I do not turn away as I undertake parting the veil of spiky vines with resolve, never mind bloody knuckles and palms.

This sulphur pong. It lights it me up. I yank the rotted rope with my ginormous hands and hoist. I balance the creaking bucket on the well's lip, cup my hands and dip in. They burn. I guzzle a draught, my lips burn. I spit a mouthful of grit back down the well's stone gullet and hear the acid hiss, the water's hissy fit.

Oh, well: I stand before your sorcery part hush-hush, part one hundred percent poison. I mutter bad memories begone into the oily suck below. Dispose of my worst trash. What I cannot save.

°

Runny boy noses and family flu shots. Dresser drawers crammed with fanned-out rows of Captain Underpants underpants. Rushed mornings of boy squabbles like fluting mourning doves. A first born's first to last driving lessons, a licence earned, a red velvet cake to celebrate. The next day, my own voice: Sure, take the keys, have a blast.

At the well's edge, I rail, mess my hair, wipe my eyes with the back of my hand and smooth my hair and shut the fuck up. I climb into the driver's seat of my tank. Sharp right, medium right, just right, a quick hi to Ivan or Isla or Ian in the guard hut.

How many rights to right wrongs?

I am still holding space for this thought when I am suddenly back in the kitchen. I reread the flyer on my fridge and put my own spin on things. Open my lips and scream out the last of what is in. A good one. A good sleep tonight. Tomorrow, who knows?

°

First thing next morning I hop out of bed and into my one-piece, skip the coffee, and fast as can be flip-flop the block to the community pool. The rose beds that edge the high white fence smudge coral and pink as I blur by, and when I arrive at the steel gate entryway it gleams, the high-flying sky above gleams too, business as usual, coin of the realm. The pool a darker, grotto blue, though I am going on memory here, as I cannot see it yet: the gate, like the fence, is a vertiginous contraption, the gate's lock is blink-you-will-miss-it tiny, for initiates only, a sliver in the silvery shine that fairly screams *only the elect enter here*. I cannot see them, but I hear my friends Kirsten and Aliyah and Alfonse and Krystal and Alain and others of their ilk ply their vigorous aquatic paths, splashing up sweet storms. I cannot wait to bring some moody their way. I wave my pass like a wand in the blue air and tap the gate. Tap, tap. A pinprick-sized light below the lock flashes red, red.

I stamp my flip-flops. I smite the gate with my fists. Never! I declare. Not in all my weirdly unspecified time here. Not what I signed on for, when I signed whatever I signed. Whatever: I understood no muss, no fuss. I might on occasion f-bomb the Community Listserv, I might middle of our starry, starry night zip my tank the wrong way along the one-ways. But I do hereby insist that I did sign on.

I pound the damned portal. I tantrum bloody knuckle prints along a goodly portion of the high white fence. Hey! HEY. Have I not seen my friends' stuff at the well? The boxes of individually wrapped umeboshi plums from the former loves of Alma's life, begging her back. The whiskers of aging companion animals, abandoned for the sake of Abdul and Kirsten's cross-country career moves.

I return to the gate and sink to the paving stones. I lie back, starfish my arms and legs, at a loss. Clear mountain air exits and enters my lungs, and I visualize myself transparent and calm as glass.

A snick-snick of the lock and the gate swings open. And who should appear but my friends Kiki and Alvin and Alma and Karina. One by one they step over me. As if I am a bag o' dirt and not someone they know, someone made of delightful blown glass, a piece they might collect, display on their pricey living room built-ins. Not their friend Darla, their Darla Doll, Darla Dear. Their iffy compatriot in this land of mostly pleasant commingling.

Hey? I whisper.

They stop as if one. They turn all together now, though it takes another full second for them to adjust their gazes and look down and notice me.

Hello?

Sound of silence. Sound of no takers.

Then Kiki beams at me. Darla Dear, we didn't see you! she says in the honeyed voice most of them use, and which I have yet to master, conflicted as I am.

See you tonight at the Community Meeting? Alma asks, so sweet of her.

It's Standards Night, Kirsten says, popping up behind the others, her tone equally dulcet.

My friend Alan appears presto-blesto from behind now—how did that happen?—bearing a split-second frown that mars his face, before he too smiles. Be there, he says with a wink. Or be more square.

I lift my hand to him, weak as a real doll. A turning point: do I not, in truth, need help?

My friend Alan reaches a forefinger toward me. Not exactly searchingly, robustly. I reach a forefinger too, and find my own digit only makes it so far, as if my batteries are running out. Help. Me. Alan's indifferent digit lands only a tap on the tip of my nose. Boop.

The prick.

I remain supine, but the hairs on my arm stand on end. As if there is life in this Darla yet.

°

Afternoon. I fix a sandwich, make coffee, pour it down the sink. Empty and wash my ice cube trays. Three thirty-three, unable to wait longer, I press the numbers on my phone. A stranger picks up, and I press piss off. Three thirty-five, the call comes through. Etna Mamoon Correctional Facility, the AI op says. This is—beep—Ruthie Lord. My identical twin's scratchy voice itches my ear. The AI op takes the reins again to say the call will be recorded, will I accept the charge?

Well?

She punched into this world a solid three minutes before me, but we shared the same placenta, her womby veins once mine too, our pinkie fingers linked on the ultrasounds. Doctors drained the excess amniotic fluid to rescue our tiny bladders, and rendered us more equals than donor and recipient, aggressor and enfeebled. But really, was there ever a question as to who was who?

How much can things, can people, really change?

I accept the charge. Ruthie talks her blue streak, six months into her three years' sentence at "the Farm"—the inmates' name for the minimum-security facility, for its grassy tree-ringed acres—where, as part of her sentence, five days a week Ruthie trains guide dogs for the blind. Juniper and Jumper are my sister's latest charges, bushy ears the size of maxi pads. During our daily calls, she fills me in on the enviable progress they make with sits and downs and comes.

I only half listen. Ruthie. Marly Marl Darla Darl: a game of dolls' thoughts, is what I am thinking, the only game of dolls I have ever permitted myself. Round and round the doll thoughts go, as if they are hair joined in braids and knots, hers and mine, mine and hers, impossible to tease them apart. For years we woke to the glitter of each other's crusted eyes. For years we grew slow as centuries, hardly milk-fed, definitely poorly fed. We possessed rumours of Mother and Father but mostly raised ourselves, wiping tears from cheeks, trading pinches to pink them to good-enough pictures of sweet and darling and dove. In time we lifted lip gloss and tampons and travel-sized tubes of hand cream from the drugstore, and always shared our spoils. Even traded off our big-girl pants when we crushed on the same wide-eyed young dudes.

My big sis: first love, first loss. A hand clamped her shoulder one day in the drugstore, and *Greatest Metal Hits* cassettes, volumes 1 and 2, clattered from her sleeves, and I bolted out the door and into passing grades at school, a job at the Mini Mart, nicer clothes, all the rest. For Ruth: foster home, a stint in juvie, stint with a guy who had impregnated his high school principal, who did time for relations with a minor and gave birth to the minor's son in a prison hospital, and this guy, no longer a minor, left Ruthie when the felonious mother of his child got out.

From there, everything. Nothing. The nothing accumulations of Ruthie's life: more petty theft, and bad cheques and bum whisky loves. Marly Marl. Whereas I, Darla Darl, married a man I met at a medical conference—having worked my way into the field of smiling at trade booths heralding medical devices that mostly worked. My husband a kind man, a famous orthopedist—a man who has fixed nearly everyone's knees and hips, joints that paid for the stately home a three days drive from here. My everything.

Everything I left. Husband and home with its sons once one, two, three. Where, on an early spring afternoon, my eldest just home from school, I said, Sure, take the keys.

I jam the phone into my ear to drown out the rising clatter and smash. I tune back in to what Ruthie is saying.

Something about Juniper and Jumper. The dogs shipping out to their new homes. Breaks Ruthie's heart, breaks her balls, her gravel-and-tar voice breaks. As if her voice is trying on the notes they will sound when she is old. If she reaches old.

I think of what will not. No ifs about it, no turnaround, conversion, no happy landing to stick. The slick of this knowledge spreads in my mind. Bubble, bubble. Smell of scorched waffles and boy funk. Muddy shoes in a mudroom and a jumble of lacrosse sticks and well-used backpacks. Hurry up, don't be late, don't forget your books.

I hurry things along with Ruthie, in a hurry to once again take my bubbling troubles to the well at dusk. I tell Ruthie I am sorry about the dogs. Sorry they will not be around to receive the gift cards I sent for them, thinking their Puppuccinos redeemable when they got out. I am sorry I had no idea what their getting out would mean.

Sorry, sorry, sorry.

Yeah, well, Ruthie says. Them's the shits.

We listen to each other breathe, as we must have when we were babes.

What I am waiting for: for Ruthie to at some point mention my missing boy. My biggest boy. Acknowledge what happened. Say she is sorry for my loss.

I wait and wait. I picture Ruthie now in best-guess snatches, having not found the time or inclination to pay her a visit at her current address. I sort of see it, the fed-issued jumpsuit. Her shoulders mounded, neck drooping. I hear the tranq slur to her laugh. Her once chestnut hair uncombed and leaking to brown at the roots. Hair I once brushed a daily hundred strokes, and plaited and coaxed into cotton candy bouffants, retro even then, and corrected into strictly marshalled sleek-straight blow-outs. The shine. The picture perfect. Funny—I have let mine go too.

Who did we think we would become, when we were girls? Chins up-thrust at the scrolling, multiple-clause clouds we tried to read once on a windy day in June.

Got to go, I tell her.

Thought as much, she says.

I do not tell her there are no more windy days in June. Not here. Where, weirdly for a mountain town, the air is always still. A giant, windless hush, an unblinking and uncanny convalescence in which there is no way to connect befores with afters. Where an ungrateful bitch might wish a storm would rush in any moment, but it never does.

Ruthie?

I am embarrassed, angry, at my voice for cracking. It makes me feel like I too have been a big fraud.

Darla?

Hey, I say. I'm sorry for your troubles. Uwaniwich too?

She cracks up. Scent of sour beloved breath, unwashed pits and cracks.

Oh, my Darl, my big sis says. My poor, darling Darl.

◦

At first, I settled in nicely. The cocktail hours that consisted of meet-ups for talks by eminent eminences on stargazing and deglazing a saucepan. I crafted a beribboned hat or three, and not a few cheery collages that I donated to the auctions at our Community Monthly Fundraiser for Those Not Like Us. At the weekly Couples Dances I paired with my friends Alan or Kira, until I learned there was no need to distinguish between them and Kristy and Kareema and Alma and Alphonse.

I bowed out whenever bird-bright voices pecked my skull. As needed, I did my business at the well. Banished spilt milk and the scorchy smell of sick-boy puke. Stepped-on Legos, begone. Piss off, car keys, and my own voice, except from far away, tinny, a thing to easily take back. I took back the astonished look on my eldest's face, as if he too were only just realizing his new life was about to unfold. My eldest, I said to him never, anticipating how that would ruin the moment and elicit fatal teenager eye-roll, which would stab my heart. My, my, my pretty, how fast you've grown, I said never. Though I did stand in the doorway and wave him safe travels.

The well in the dark glade, these perfect streets. The long-range high-alt views, air cool and clean, and everyone got up all nice, not too wealthy selfie, not too sad meh. Everyone waving at everyone else all the time. Waving at each other's nice outfits from our luxury sporty tanks, waving at each other in our fine swimsuits at the Community pool. I'm good, I'm good too, never anything but goods. Everyone's weed-free beds of lobelia and foxglove and backyard grills gleaming. You good? Sure am. Not a speck of dirt or thought out of place. Except at my place. The perfect got to me. Or I wanted to stand out, display a goblin-mode tangle within, like the spindly honeysuckle sucking the roots of my wrecked rose beds, prowling upward for the remaining frail buds. I wanted to score a prize for worst hurt. Which proves I do take a certain pride. The problem is, my derelictions result in my friends putting a finer, nosier point on the old, Hey, how you doing?

How I am doing: in danger of the big boot.

°

The Community Center, lit by low floodlights, resembles a spaceship. Plunked down, it occurs to me, to superintend the chosen. I take a seat in the back row of the meeting hall. From what I can tell from the back, everyone who is anyone is already here. The meeting commences, led by my friends Kira and Alan, who speak into microphones from the table set up in front. I love looking at them, and the lanternflies that circle the hall lights, which Alan and Kira do not seem to notice, too busy scanning the lucent faces before them, faces I am unable to see, but can well imagine, seeing them every day, as I do. A lanternfly lands on the shoulder of the woman seated in front of me, a shapely bewinged shoulder. The man to my left, woman to my right: same thing, a lanternfly for each.

We reach the point in the meeting where Kira and Alan say, Raise your hand. Which they say as if one. Step up to the microphones in the aisle, they say.

Hands rise, voices float through the sound system. It is possible I space. It is possible that, when I come to, a lanternfly lands on a man's head three rows up.

Anyone else? Alan and Kira say.

My turn. I raise my hand. I make my way to a mic.

Hello? I whisper. Can you all hear me?

The sound is soft and ragged as ancient claws. The moth-flies arise, loop lopsided orbits beneath the ceiling. The audience turns, as if one in their seats, toward me.

Why, Darla Doll, Alan intones like a god from his seat on the dais.

Why, Dear Darl, Kira says, voice belling as if from a tower.

Then they speak faster, over each other, repeating themselves until their voices merge. An answering chorus rises from the floor, an echo as if from a deep well, a different well than the one I know. The sound chirring, insectoidal, an unsound sound that bears little resemblance to my name. *We love you, we love you, we love you.*

I have never been so weirded out. So afraid. Almost never.

Full disclosure time, what I have not previously braved. I gnarl my fists around the mic stand and open, really open, my filthy mouth.

My pretties, I garble. I have tried, but I cannot love you all.

The echo picks up, a metallic reverb. My friends' faces craze with frowns.

I fling my arms wide.

The truth? I say. For real real? I cannot love you at all.

°

Blocks away, I slow my roll past the faux Tudors and French-farmhouse-influenced and quasi-mid-centuries. My phone pings:

a group text from Kira-Kiril, Alma-Alan. We love you, we love you. I kick off my mid-heels and abandon them on the sidewalk. Mount a neighbour's immaculate lawn, tear through the hellebores, scale a fence, and wreak a jagged path among pastel poolside loungers. A waxing gibbous tonight, my fave. The night-dyed crepe myrtles and honey locusts wave me on, and deep in the branches of not a few I spy the ghosty, silken mats of tent caterpillars. I wave, pump my fist, all hail to the despoilers. The very thought tinkles prettily in my cold, dead heart.

°

I take stock. Real moths adjourn in my every closet, raddling my pretty clothes and bed linens with holes. The smell of rot and toothpaste suffuses the first-floor powder room. My phone rings and rings and I stuff it under a couch cushion and lie down on the living room floor. Above me, three picture frames rest face down on the console. In one, my husband the famous orthopedist. I close my eyes, and he wavers in my mind as if standing in a steady rain. I hold him in the rain, until he dissolves into a faraway sleep on a cot in a hallway in a country I have in my steadfast ignorance never heard of, his SAT phone recharging on the floor next to him. It is late and he is asleep, and then he wakes, and then my phone rings. I dig it out from under the couch cushion. I press accept, and it is my husband, newly given over to a life in service to those who most need his services, this newly reconstituted husband calling on his SAT phone. He asks how I am doing. He asks if I know about the storm back home, power out for a week. He asks if I know how the remaining boy and boy are doing, sleeved and bandaged into boarding school uniforms, how they are doing at swim and sad poetry class. Do I know if boy and boy would like a dog to come home to at the start of summer break? He asks if I would like a dog. Would I like a dog and two boys? Would I like him, my husband, to return home?

Well, I say. Well, I'm fine, I'm good, thanks for asking. Hope you're sleeping okay. A dog and two boys sound okay too. At this point.

He does not ask at what point, what I mean by that. He says, Okay, good. Would you like to talk again, next Wednesday, is that okay?

A small one, I say.

What's that?

A small dog.

Sure, he says.

I am embarrassed that I have no idea which day next Wednesday will be, when it will come. I am afraid to ask. Afraid of my privilege, my luck.

Love you, he says.

What's that? I say. Wait, what?

I feel as if my head is draining liquid, a reverse guzzle drying me out, and it is a shock to my system that I can see what is left.

Sprays of milk teeth. Captain Underpants underpants in dresser drawers. An eldest's first full day as a licenced driver—so suddenly all grown-up, then suddenly not. My husband's strong arms and hands that have done everyone's knees and hips, and snugged around me in bed on the nights I could stand to stay in bed. Could stand to not find fault and accept this new and reduced us. Regard it as changing weather, iffy times. My poor husband. The torn faces of remaining boy and boy, the younger two, stuffed into deck shoes and knit ties, and shouty swim team for after-school hours. Boy and boy. The hard candy of their hearts that, in my acid absence, my retiring to this mountain stronghold, I have sucked to nothing.

I could call my husband. I could offer to speak to my boys. This much is clear.

◦

I wake damned tired on the living room floor. Morning. My phone pings from the couch. A scratchy sound issues from my entryway. I rouse to a slew of group texts, discover a letter slid under my oak door. I rip the flap on the envelope with the gold-embossed conifer ringed by mountains. Another chance, the missive says, a repeat of what's on my phone. A clean slate. Darla Doll, we love you.

Repeat, repeat: a seduction of ever-tightening rings, squeezing until there is no point to me. No remaining boy and boy waving stick-figure arms, no husband waving. No sister I once shared a mattress with, a placenta, pinkie fingers hooked.

I shred the letter, hit delete on the texts. Erase the Community contacts on my phone and hop over to the Community socials. Unfriend, unfriend. Boop.

◦

Late morning, I throw together a rosé cooler, ditch my clothes, and slide open the sliding glass door to my backyard patio, where I park my bare tush on the rusty chaise longue. A lanternfly wings around me, wings not exactly gossamer, but they will do. The short-range view rises to my left, and to my right, the long:

every which way, mountains unending. I polish my drink. The sun angles lower. A wind springs up. Wind, imagine that. I am one giant goose pimple, my head something a giant might pop. My roof rattles, a slate tile flips loose and detonates by my toes and chips another chip in the bluestone. Inside, my craft room remains empty of anything that can reassemble anything resembling my former life. Any life, period.

I, Darla Doll—a reject deepfake—draw my bare, freezing legs to my chin. My mature hemlocks toss in the now-growing twilight, the shrubbery cowers. An owl hoots, as if right on cue. I blink or I space and the now-night sky clouds over, a cataract gleam. My accent lights flash on. Moths, real ones, descend like huge snowflakes.

I close my eyes.

Oh, well: your witchery. Your bewitching beauty of terrible wishes.

Can a person miss what's never happened? In light of what has.

Call it longing. Days when mist shrouds the peaks. When a cool, clear night surrenders to freak thunderstorm. At dawn a fog you can cup in your hand and eat.

A bird that worries the trees—no, three. My pretties. They hop to the patchy grass and pluck worms, rosy and plump, from the ground.

Morning. I touch my hair, lit with dew.

ACKNOWLEDGEMENTS

Stories from *Big of You* have appeared in a slightly different form in the following:

"Arnhem" in *Best Canadian Stories 2021*, the first part of "Cooler" in *Best Canadian Stories 2024*, the entirety of "Cooler" in *The Hopkins Review*, "Once Then Suddenly Later" in *Copper Nickel*, "Return to Forever" in *Camel*, and "Sounds Like" in *Camel*.

Thank you to Dan Wells, Vanessa Stauffer, Ashley Van Elswyk, and the rest of the wonderful team at Biblioasis.

Thank you to Ingrid Paulson for the fab cover and interior design.

Thank you to Danielle Evans, Alejandro Heredia, Cynthia Holz, Clarissa Hurley, Mark Jarman, Erika Krouse, Joanna Luloff, Dora Malech, Lisa Moore, and Diane Schoemperlen.

Thank you Susie Brandt and Karen Houppert.

Thank you to the Canada Council for the Arts, for generous support during the writing of this book.

I remain grateful beyond words to John Metcalf, for his love of words worth reaching for.

Vid Smooke: all hats off and loving awe for your shared expertise in all things music as well as words. I'm still so glad you waved *very* effusively at me across a snowy parking lot in New Hampshire 29 years ago.

ELISE LEVINE is the author, most recently, of *Say This: Two Novellas*, the story collection *This Wicked Tongue*, and the novel *Blue Field*. Her work has appeared in *Ploughshares*, *Copper Nickel*, *Blackbird*, *The Walrus*, and five times in *Best Canadian Stories*. She lives in Baltimore, where she teaches in the MA in Writing program at Johns Hopkins University.